PACK OF WOLVES

PACK OF WOLVES

by Vasil Bykov

translated from the Russian by
Lynn Solotaroff

THOMAS Y. CROWELL   NEW YORK

Translated from the Russian by Lynn Solotaroff
For information address Thomas Y. Crowell Junior Books, 10 East 53rd Street,
New York, N. Y. 10022. Published simultaneously in Canada by
Fitzhenry & Whiteside Limited, Toronto.
Designed by Joyce Hopkins

Library of Congress Cataloging in Publication Data

Bykov, Vasil', 1924–
Pack of wolves.
SUMMARY: In the forests of Belorussia in 1942, a group
of disabled Russian partisans makes its way to a medical
unit while being pursued by German soldiers.
    [1. World War, 1939–1945—Soviet Union—Fiction.
2. Soviet Union—Fiction] I. Title.
PZ7.B988Pac   1981   [Fic]   80-2456
ISBN 0-690-04114-4   ISBN 0-690-04115-2 (lib. bdg.)   AACR2

1 2 3 4 5 6 7 8 9 10
First Edition

PACK OF WOLVES

1

Together with a dense crowd of people, Levchuk squeezed through the open iron gates of the railroad station. He found himself on a large square filled with cars. Here the passengers from the train that had just pulled in began to disperse, and he slowed his pace. He had no idea what direction to take—whether to follow the street leading from the station into town, or head for the two yellow buses awaiting passengers at the other end of the square. Undecided, he stopped, put his old, metal-braced suitcase down on the hot, oil-stained pavement, and took a look around. He had better ask for directions. The address was written on a crumpled envelope in his pocket, but he already knew it by heart, and so he began staring at passersby, trying to decide whom to approach.

At that late afternoon hour, there were plenty of people in the square, but they looked so hurried or preoccupied as they passed that he stood for a while in uncertainty before going over to a fairly elderly man, like himself, who was unfolding a paper he had just bought at the newsstand.

"Could you tell me how to get to Cosmonaut Street, please? Can I walk, or do I have to take a bus?"

The man looked up from his newspaper with what seemed to Levchuk a not very pleased expression, and shot a look at him through his glasses. He didn't answer right away. Either he was trying to remember the street or was scrutinizing this stranger, obviously an out-of-towner, who was dressed in a crumpled gray jacket and a dark blue shirt which, despite the heat, was buttoned up to the neck.

Under the man's searching gaze, Levchuk regretted that he hadn't put on the tie which had been hanging, unused, for years on a special nail in the closet. He hated knotting ties and was no good at it, so he had dressed for the trip as he would for his days off at home: in a gray, fairly new suit and a nylon shirt. (The shirt had been fashionable long

2

ago when he'd bought it; this was the first time he'd put it on.) Here, however, all the men were dressed differently—either in light, short-sleeved T-shirts, or, probably because it was a day off, in white shirts and ties. But, he decided, it didn't matter much. He'd get along all right as he was. He had more important things to worry about than his appearance.

"Cosmonaut Street . . . Cosmonaut Street," the man repeated, as though trying to recall the street, and he glanced around. "Take the number seven bus over there. When you get to the square, cross the street to the food store and transfer to the number eleven. Go two stops on that and then ask again. It's only about half a mile from there."

"Thanks," said Levchuk, though not much of this had registered. Since he didn't want to detain this man, he merely asked, "Is it far? About three miles?"

"Three? No more than a mile and a half."

"Well, I can manage that on foot," Levchuk said, delighted that the street he wanted was closer than he'd originally thought.

He set off along the pavement at a leisurely pace, trying not to bump into people with his suitcase. They moved along in groups of twos and threes, young and old, all obviously in a hurry, and all, for some reason, coming toward him. There were

3

even more people near a food store he passed, and when he peered through the bright windows, he was surprised to see a crowd of customers swarming like bees around the counter. It seemed as if some holiday or big event in town was approaching. He picked up snatches of conversation, but could make nothing out of them, and walked on until he saw a huge sign with the word FOOTBALL written on it in orange. When he got closer he read an announcement of a game that was to take place that day, and, somewhat surprised, realized the cause of all the activity in the streets.

He himself had practically no interest in football and seldom watched the games on television—he felt that football might be good entertainment for children and young people, or for those who played the game, but that for sensible elderly people, it lacked seriousness, amounted to kids' stuff.

The people in this town, however, obviously had a different attitude toward the game. It became difficult for him to make any headway walking, and the less time that remained until kickoff, the greater the crush became. Buses crammed with people crawled past, some of the passengers draped around doors the drivers couldn't shut, while most of the buses going the other way were empty.

To avoid pestering people with questions, Levchuk kept glancing at the corner houses with the street names on them until he spotted one with the long-awaited words COSMONAUT STREET written on a blue slab. There was no number on it, so he went on to the next building; there he saw that the one he wanted was still some distance away. He walked on, observing the life of this big city he had never been in before and probably would not have visited now, had it not been for the good news he'd received from his nephew. True, the boy hadn't communicated anything more than the address, had not even made inquiries to find out where or what Victor's job was, or what kind of family he had. But what could one expect of a first-year student who had stumbled on the familiar name in a newspaper and, at Levchuk's request, had looked up Victor's address in the local registry office? He would find out about all this himself now—that was what he had come for.

Above all, it was a joy to know that Victor had survived the war. Levchuk hoped fate had treated him more kindly since. If he lived on such a prosperous-looking block, he couldn't be just a nobody; he might even be some sort of official. This idea gave Levchuk a sense of pride.

As he looked up at the big buildings with their light brick facades and numerous balconies, many of them cluttered with articles (beach boards, deck chairs, little tables and boxes, various odds and ends tied up in clothesline), he tried to imagine Victor's apartment. Naturally, it too would have a balcony and be on a high floor. Levchuk believed that the higher the floor, the better the apartment—it would have more sun and air. Above all, there would be a good view, and you'd be able to see the whole town, or at least half of it. About six years before, he'd visited his sister-in-law in Kharkov and had very much enjoyed sitting on the balcony in the evenings, even though the apartment had only been on the third floor of a ten-story building.

It would be interesting to see what kind of reception he would get.

At first, of course, he would knock—not very loudly or persistently, not with his fist, but with the tips of his fingers, as his wife had instructed him before he left. And when the door opened, he would take a step back. It might be better to take his cap off beforehand—perhaps in the entrance or on the stairs. When the door opened, he would first ask whether the person he wanted was living there. It would be a good thing if Victor himself came to the door. Levchuk would probably recognize him, even though thirty years had passed, enough time for anyone to change beyond recognition. All the same, he would doubtless recognize him. He had known his father well, and Victor must bear some resemblance to him. If his wife or one of the children were to open—No, the children were probably too young. Still, they might not be—why shouldn't a five- or six-year-old child come to the door to greet a guest? If one of them did, he would give his name and ask for the head of the household.

Then, he felt, the most important and most difficult moment would come. He already knew how wonderful and yet disturbing it was to meet someone you had known long ago. You would suddenly be filled with memories, and amazement, and a sense of awkwardness at discovering that the person you had known and remembered was not the stranger standing before you, but another. . . .

Most likely they'd invite him in. Naturally they'd have a fine apartment with gleaming parquet floors, sofas, carpets—as good as any of the apartments in town these days. He'd leave his suitcase at the door and remove his shoes. That was something he must remember to do, since he'd heard it had become the custom in town. He was wearing new socks, which he'd bought in the village store before leaving for a ruble sixty-six kopecks, so he need not be embarrassed by them.

Then, of course, they would have a talk, and it wouldn't be an easy one. However much he'd thought about it, he just couldn't imagine how they'd begin. But he'd see when the time came.

Probably they'd ask him to dinner, and he'd walk over to his suitcase and get out the big bottle with the foreign label on it that had been gurgling quietly all through his trip, and the little country treats he had brought along. People in town had plenty of food these days, but a ring of country sausage, a jar of honey, and a pair of smoked bream (he had caught the fish himself) would not be at all amiss at his host's table.

Lost in thought, Levchuk walked farther than he should have and found himself at number eighty-eight instead of seventy-eight. Annoyed with himself, he turned back, walked quickly past a little garden and a building with a huge sign, HAIR-DRESSER, along the entire ground floor, and caught sight of number seventy-six at the corner. For a minute he stared at it in bewilderment, wondering what had happened to all the buildings between eighty-eight and seventy-six. Just then he heard a polite little voice at his side.

"What building are you looking for, *dyadya*?"*

Two little girls were standing behind him on the sidewalk. One of them, about eight years old and with flaxen hair, was twirling a net bag with a carton of milk in it, and she looked up at him trustingly. The other, dark-haired and slightly taller than her

---

* *Dyadya* means "uncle"; it is a term Russian children use to address an older man.

friend, was dressed in boy's shorts and licking an ice cream wrapper in paper. She stood there observing him more cautiously.

"I want number seventy-eight. Do you know where it is?"

"Seventy-eight? Yes, but which group of buildings is it?"

"Which group?"

This was the first he'd heard about a group of buildings. He'd simply noticed the numbers of the building and the apartment. What was all this about a group?

To be sure he hadn't made a mistake, he put down his suitcase, which felt rather heavy by now, and took the crumpled envelope with the address on it out of his inner pocket. Sure enough, following the building number was the figure three, and then the apartment number.

"This must be it, yes. Group three, it seems."

The two girls looked at the envelope together, to confirm the group, and told him they knew where the building was.

"It's where that mean Nelka lives, the building behind the sandbox," said the dark-haired girl with the ice cream. "We'll show you."

Feeling somewhat embarrassed, he followed them. The girls turned at the next corner, and they came to a huge courtyard. It was surrounded by several five-story buildings separated by trampled playgrounds and rows of newly planted trees. Women were sitting and chatting on benches, a volleyball game was in progress between two buildings, and some small boys were chasing each other around on bicycles. There seemed to be children everywhere—running, shouting, playing. As the girls walked beside him, the smaller one looked up at Levchuk and asked, "Why do you have only one arm, *dyadya?*"

Her friend broke in with a whisper. "How can you ask such a thing, Irka? It musta been blown off in the war. Wasn't it, *dyadya?*"

"Right, right. You're a sharp little girl."

"*Dyadya* Kolya lives in our yard and he's got only one leg. The Germans blew the other one off. He goes around in a little car. A tiny car, just a little taller than a motorbike."

"The Fascists killed my grandpa in the war," the smaller girl, Irka, informed him with a sigh.

"They wanted to kill everyone, but our soldiers wouldn't let them. Isn't that right, *dyadya?*"

"Right," he said with a smile. The smaller one ran ahead and then turned back to him, still twirling the net bag with the milk in it.

"*Dyadya,* have you got any medals? My grandpa had six."

"Six! Well, that's very good!" he said. "Means your grandpa was a real hero."

"Are you a hero too?" the little one persisted, squinting comically in the sun.

"Me? A hero? No, I'm no hero."

"There's the building," the dark-haired one said, pointing across a row of young lime trees to a building that, like all the others around, was made of gray brick. "Group three."

"Well, thank you, girls. Thanks a lot!" he said, quite moved.

The two girls sang out a simultaneous "You're welcome!" and ran off down a path.

Feeling suddenly agitated, Levchuk slowed his pace. So here he was! For some reason he wanted to put off for a while this coming meeting with the person he'd been thinking and reminiscing about all these thirty long years. But he mastered his ill-timed cowardice. Now that he'd come, he must at least have a look, say hello, and convince himself that he wasn't mistaken, that this was the Victor Platonov who meant so much to him.

He went first to the corner of the building and compared the number of the envelope with the one painted in orange on the rough brick wall. The girls were right, this was indeed group three. He put the envelope back in his pocket, buttoned it, and picked up his suitcase. Now he'd have to find the apartment, and that might not be easy in this huge building, which appeared to contain a hundred or more apartments.

Looking to one side and then the other, Levchuk proceeded somewhat hesitantly to the first entrance, accidentally frightening away a gray cat that had been sprawling lazily in a flower bed. Before opening the door, he read a notice on it listing the zone number and instructing tenants to turn off all electrical appliances before leaving their apartments. He also read an announcement of a tenants' meeting to discuss provisions for various services for the buildings. Over the door was a metal plate indicating the entrance and the numbers of the apartments within. They ranged from one to twenty, which meant that the one he wanted wasn't here. He moved on, passing the next entrance and going to the third.

Two old ladies were seated by the door. They were warmly dressed despite the heat, one actually wearing felt boots, the other holding a cane pressed firmly against the pavement. They broke off their hushed conversation and looked up at him attentively, obviously expecting a question. But he already knew what to look for and where, and so, with a slight feeling of awkwardness, he stepped past them and glanced up at the plate over the door. Yes, he was in the right place, the apartment he wanted was here. Aware of his heart pounding, he pushed the door open with his foot and stepped inside.

On the first floor were five apartments, numbers forty to forty-four, and he went slowly up to the next floor, passing a blue box with rows of numbered slots in it from which the corners of newspapers protruded. Noticing the numbers, he realized that fifty-two must be one floor above.

On the next landing he had to pause for breath; he wasn't accustomed to steep climbs and felt winded. Besides, he couldn't rid himself of a growing sense of uneasiness—it was as though he were about to make a tiresome request or were guilty of something. No matter how many times he had tried to reassure himself, he realized that this meeting would have to be somewhat upsetting for himself as well as for Victor.

The door to number fifty-two turned out to be on the left side of the landing, and, like all the others, it was painted and had a mat placed neatly in front of it and a number written above. He put his suitcase down, took a breath, and, struggling to overcome his hesitancy, quietly tapped at the door with the tips of his fingers. Then, after waiting a bit, he tapped again. He seemed to hear the sounds of voices, but when he listened more closely, he realized that they were coming from a radio. When he knocked a third time, the door of the adjacent apartment opened.

"Why don't you ring?" said a woman hurriedly

wiping her hands on her apron. While he was study-
ing the door, searching for the bell, she came over
and pressed a tiny black button on the doorjamb.
Three piercing rings sounded, but still no one came
to the door.

"They must be out," the woman said. "The little
girl was playing around here in the morning, but
I haven't seen her since. They must have gone somewhere in town."

Discouraged by his failure, Levchuk leaned back
against the banister wearily. Somehow it had never
occurred to him that they might not be home, might
go off somewhere. Yet it was perfectly understandable. After all, did he himself sit home all day?
Even now, when he was retired?

Apparently there was nothing he could do. He
couldn't wait forever on the landing, so he headed
downstairs. Before closing her door, the neighbor
called out to him, "I almost forgot, there's a football
game today. I expect they may be there."

Perhaps, he thought, *or perhaps they've gone
somewhere else.* There were plenty of things to do
in town on a nice day off—go to the park, the movies, a restaurant, the theater. There was no lack
of interesting things to do here, it wasn't like the
country. Surely he hadn't been fool enough to think
Victor would sit home thirty years waiting for his
visit?

He tramped down the six rather steep flights of stairs and walked out of the building. The old ladies broke off their conversation again and stared at him with heightened interest. By this time he no longer felt awkward, and he stopped at the edge of the path, trying to figure out what to do next. Probably the thing to do was wait, particularly since he wanted to sit for a while and stretch his legs after his long walk from the station. He glanced around and noticed an empty stone bench in a shady corner of the courtyard, and walked slowly, wearily toward it.

After wearily putting his suitcase down, Levchuk took a seat and stretched his aching feet with pleasure, cursing himself for having listened to his wife and put on a new pair of shoes. It would have been better to have come in his old worn ones. He wanted to take his shoes off, but was embarrassed to do that here—there were people all around, and children playing in the sandbox. In a garage a little distance away two men had the hood of a Moskvich* up and were tinkering with the engine.

He had a good view of the entrance where the old ladies were sitting, and he could easily see people who went through the door. He felt he would recog-

* The Moskvich is a popular Soviet-made car.

nize the tenants of number fifty-two as soon as they showed up. So he decided to stay put and wait for Victor here. It was fairly peaceful, not too hot in the shade, and he could while away the time by watching all the people.

Admittedly, every now and then his thoughts would revert to the war, to those two days in his life as a partisan that had ultimately brought him here. He had no need to strain his memory, even though he was no longer young. He remembered everything that had happened then, down to the smallest detail, as if it had been yesterday. Thirty years had not dulled anything.

He had recalled and pondered the events of those days many times. Some things gave him a modest sense of pride, but others aroused a belated feeling of embarrassment and even annoyance with himself for the person he had been then. Still, it had been the war. He had been young and not much inclined to consider the meaning of his actions, which, for the most part, had amounted to only one thing: trying to kill the enemy, and avoiding getting killed himself. . . .

2

In those days events took their own special course, and one led a mean, hungry, dangerous life. After five days and nights spent fighting off the German mop-up troops that were hemming them in, Levchuk and his comrade were utterly exhausted. Levchuk desperately wanted to sleep. . . .

No sooner had he dozed off under a fir tree than someone called him. The voice sounded familiar, and his sleep lightened and almost lifted completely. But it had such a powerful hold on him that instead of waking he remained in a nether land between oblivion and reality.

Every now and then a sense of the very real dangers in the forest broke through—the snapping of branches in the undergrowth; fragments of a conversation; the sounds of muffled but none-too-distant firing, which had not ceased since the first day of the siege. But Levchuk stubbornly deceived himself into believing that he heard nothing, and went on sleeping, refusing to rouse himself. He simply had to get another two hours' sleep, at the very least one. And he felt that he had earned the right to this sleep, which no one could deprive him of now: not the master sergeant, or the company commander, or even the commander of the detachment—no one but the Germans.

Levchuk had been wounded.

He had been wounded toward evening, soon after the company had beaten back the fourth attack of the day, and the Germans, after dragging their dead and wounded from the marsh, had quieted down a bit. Probably they were awaiting an order that their senior command had been slow to come through with, for it frequently happened that after four unsuccessful attacks, a commander would feel the need to think things over before ordering a fifth. . . .

As he sat in his shallow trench crisscrossed with roots, Levchuk, who had grown wise by now in the arts of war, surmised that the enemy had worn itself out, and that his company was going to get a breather. After waiting a little while longer, he placed the heavy butt of his machine gun on the parapet and took from his pocket a crust of bread left over from the day before. Keeping a watchful eye on the narrow strip of woodland ahead, he chewed the bread. When his hunger had abated a little, he felt the need for a smoke—but as luck would have it, he had run out of tobacco. After listening closely for a moment, he called out to his neighbor, seated close by in a similar sandy trench from which the pungent smell of homegrown tobacco wafted across in the quiet evening air.

"Kisel! Toss me a butt!"

After a while Kisel threw him one, but his aim proved none too good, and the cleft stick into which he'd inserted the butt landed short of Levchuk's trench. With some apprehension, Levchuk reached out for it. But he couldn't get hold of it and made a second try, leaning halfway out of the trench. Just then a rifle shot rang out not far across the marsh, something snapped under his arm, and pine needles and dry sand lashed his face. Dropping the ill-fated butt, Levchuk darted back into his trench, unaware at first of a sudden warmth in his sleeve. He was amazed to see a small bullet hole in the shoulder of his jacket.

"Bastards!"

What a damned nuisance to have gotten

wounded, and in such a stupid way. But wounded he was, and apparently seriously. Blood soon began to stream heavily down his fingers and he felt a stiff, biting sensation in his shoulder. Sinking lower in his trench and swearing, Levchuk bandaged up his shoulder with the soiled cotton rag he had used to wrap his bread in, and gritted his teeth. After a few minutes the nasty implications of this wound sank in and Levchuk became furious with himself for his carelessness, and even more furious with those across the marsh. As the pain in his shoulder grew stronger, he grabbed his machine gun, intending to send a raking burst of fire through the willows where the Germans had been lying in wait for him. But instead of firing, he let out a suppressed scream. The pressure of the gun against his shoulder caused such excruciating pain that he immediately realized he was no longer fit to be a machine gunner. Keeping well down in his trench, he called out again to Kisel.

"Tell the company commander I'm wounded! Hear? Wounded!"

Luckily it was growing dark, and after the long sultry day the sun was sinking below the horizon. The marsh was veiled in a thin, gauzelike mist that it was difficult to see through. The Germans still were not beginning their fifth attack. When it became a little darker, Mezhevich, the company commander, came running over to the ridge of pines.

"What's this? Wounded?" he asked. He dropped down on the dry pine needles and peered into the misty air over the marsh. A stench of gunpowder drifted across to them in the cool evening air.

"Yes, here—in the shoulder."

"Right one?"

"Yes."

"Well, then," said the commander, "off to see Paikin. Give your gun to Kisel."

"What? Some machine gunner he is!"

At first Levchuk felt insulted by the order. To give his beautifully kept gun to a country boy like Kisel, who couldn't even handle a rifle properly, meant being put on the same level with him, and Levchuk didn't like that. Only the best of the partisans, former Red Army men, were chosen to be machine gunners. But the truth was that there were no Red Army men left, and the gun had to be turned over to someone.

With a deliberate show of indifference, Levchuk carried his weapon over to Kisel's trench alongside the next pine tree. Then he moved on into the depths of the woods until he came to a stream. This was the location of both the supply base of the besieged sector, and the medical unit run by Verkhovets and Paikin—"death's assistants," as the partisans jokingly called them. In part there were reasons for this—Paikin had worked only as a dentist prior to the war, and Verkhovets had probably never even held a bandage in his hands before. But there was no one better to be found here, and so the two of them treated the men, changed their dressings, and sometimes even amputated arms or legs.

Several wounded men were already sitting alongside the stream by the medical unit. Levchuk waited his turn. In the dim light Paikin somehow managed to clean up his bloody shoulder with stinging peroxide and bandage it up tightly with a strip of linen.

"Stick your arm in your belt and keep it there. It's nothing serious. You'll be slinging a sledgehammer in a week."

Everyone knows that an encouraging word from a doctor sometimes does more good than medicine. Levchuk immediately felt the pain in his shoulder subside, and he decided that when morning came he would go back to his company. Meanwhile, he'd get some sleep. He wanted to sleep now more than anything in the world.

Levchuk dozed off again under the fir tree, sitting on its rough, knotty roots. But he soon became aware of a trampling of boots, the sounds of voices, and the creaking of a cart nearby. He recognized Paikin's voice, and the voice of the new chief of staff, and that of still another person he knew, though he was too sleepy to identify it.

"I won't go! I'm not going anywhere!"

Of course! It was Klava Shorokhina, the detachment radio operator. Levchuk could have told her voice from a hundred others half a mile away, and now she was within ten feet of him. He came to immediately, though he still couldn't quite get his eyes open. He moved his shoulder under his padded jacket and held his breath.

"What do you mean, you're not going? Think we're going to open up a maternity hospital for you?" growled their new chief of staff, until recently commander of No. 1 Company. "Paikin!"

"Here, Comrade Commander!"

"Ship her off! Ship her off at once with Tikhonov. They'll get to Yazminki somehow and can spend time at the medical unit in the May Day Brigade."

"I won't go!" Klava cried again in a voice full of desperation and hopelessness.

"Listen, Shorokhina," Paikin interceded gently. "You can't stay here. You yourself said your time was coming."

"Well, let it!"

"Damn it, you'll get killed!" raged the chief of staff. "We're going to have to crawl out on our bellies to break out of here. Understand that?"

"Let them kill me!"

" 'Let them kill me!' Did you hear that? They ought to have killed you earlier!"

An awkward pause followed, broken only by Klava's quiet sobbing and the sound of the medical unit driver urging on his horse in the distance: "Get a move on, you miserable bitch!" It seemed as if the supply units were beginning to stir, but Levchuk still didn't rouse himself, still didn't even open his eyes. He just continued to listen.

"Paikin!" the chief of staff commanded. "Get them into the cart and send them off! Send them with Levchuk! He'll keep an eye out for trouble. But where is he? You said he was here?"

"He was, I bandaged him up."

That's the end of my sleep, thought Levchuk disconsolately. He didn't move, hoping they'd call someone else.

"Levchuk! Hey, Levchuk! Griboyed, where is he?"

"He was sleeping somewhere nearby, I saw him," said the medical unit driver. Levchuk swore under his breath. *He saw me! Why'd he have to say that?*

"Go and find him," the chief of staff ordered. "Put Tikhonov on the cart and take the brushwood road—before they close it up. Levchuk!" the chief shouted.

"Here I am. What do you want?" Levchuk replied with irritation as he scrambled up from under the fir tree.

It was pitch black and he couldn't see a thing,

but from the scattered sounds he picked up, the muffled voices of the partisans, the general stir of activity, Levchuk realized that the camp was on the move. Carts were being hauled out from under the fir trees and the drivers were harnessing their horses. Someone moved close by him, and Levchuk could tell from the swish of his long army cape that it was the chief of staff.

"Levchuk! You know the brushwood road by the swamp?"

"Of course."

"Get moving, then. Get Tikhonov out or he'll be done for. Take him to the May Day Brigade. By the brushwood road. Reconnaissance says there's a loophole, you can still get through."

"Damn it all!" retorted Levchuk. "Why should I go to May Day? I want to go back to my own company!"

"How can you? You're wounded. Paikin, where did he get hit?"

"In the shoulder, a direct hit."

"You see? So get a move on. Take the brushwood road. The cart is under your command. And . . . also take Klava."

Paikin's voice broke in from the darkness.

"Klava ought to go to a village where there's a midwife. An experienced woman."

"A midwife!" Levchuk shot back at him irritably.

He turned away, adjusting the stiff leather holster of his German Luger, which had been pressing against his ribs. "As if I didn't have better things to do."

. . . As for Klava, he'd known about her condition, but had never dreamed he'd be saddled with the job of finding her a midwife! While they'd all be trying to break through, he'd have to drive God knows where, and with such a crew—the half-senile Griboyed, the pregnant Klava, and that goner Tikhonov. When Levchuk had come in that evening, he'd noticed the paratrooper lying beside the first-aid tent; he'd been covered with some sacking and his bandaged head had stuck out like a chopping block. His eyes had also been bandaged, and he hadn't even moved, had seemed not to be breathing. Levchuk had walked past him with a vague sense of alarm, thinking that the paratrooper had probably made his last jump. And that girl Klava . . . There'd been a time when Levchuk would have been honored to drive an extra half mile in the woods with her, but not now. Klava didn't interest him now.

How much trouble this damned wound was causing him! And by the look of things, it would continue to do so. The May Day Brigade mightn't be so far, but just try getting there with the Fascists blockading the road. The scouts had said there was a loophole. *But who can tell where it is? And what kind of loophole?* Levchuk reasoned, shivering in the damp night air. He wished he hadn't given Kisel his machine gun or reported to the medical unit.

He intended to have it out with the chief of staff and go back to his company. The company commander most likely wouldn't turn him back, and he'd be fighting again with the others instead of tramping off God only knows where. But by the time he'd made up his mind, there was no one to protest to. The chief had walked off, and the swish of his army cape was no longer audible in the bushes. Paikin had disappeared into the darkness even before. Close by a horse was thumping the shafts with its tail, and Griboyed, the driver, was stamping around trying to adjust its harness. Klava waited off to the side, sobbing quietly. Paying no attention to them, Levchuk swore: "Damn those commanders! What asses! The hell with them all!"

3

They drove through the forest in pitch blackness.

From time to time the cart almost overturned in the ruts and potholes there, while branches beat relentlessly against the cart and lashed its riders. Levchuk kept his head down and protected his wounded shoulder under his jacket. After the first fifteen minutes or so, he had no idea where they were going. Luckily Griboyed seemed to know the area and didn't ask for directions. The horse was finding it rough going, but they seemed to be on the right road. Still seething with anger, Levchuk remained silent and listened to the rumble of gunfire on every side. Sometimes a flare went up, and its quivering light hovered over the treetops in the distance.

After forcing their way through the thick scrub, they finally drove out onto a forest road. The cart moved along more easily, and Levchuk settled in more comfortably, squeezing in beside the motionless body of the paratrooper Tikhonov, who seemed to be unconscious or asleep. Levchuk quietly reached for the barrel of the man's submachine gun, which was making him uncomfortable. But as soon as he got a firm grip on it, Tikhonov grabbed it away and held tightly to the barrel.

"N—no! Hands off!"

"Damn you!" thought Levchuk.

Levchuk would have liked to take possession of that gun, because he sensed it would soon come in handy. They were hardly likely to avoid running into Germans on this road. And he had only his Luger with two clips of cartridges, and Griboyed a rifle flung over his back. Possibly Klava also had a gun. But altogether, it wasn't much to get them through the fifteen miles they had to travel to the May Day Brigade, particularly if there were Germans in the immediate vicinity. Which was more than likely. How could they possibly have laid siege to the sector and left the brushwood road open? What difference did it make if the scouts said there was a loophole?

Having thought it over, Levchuk nudged Griboyed's elbow. "Stop!" he said.

The driver drew up the horse and listened intently. Far behind them there was the sound of firing, but close by it was quiet. They could distinctly hear the tired breathing of the horse and the rustling of the bushes in the night wind.

"Is the brushwood road still far?" Levchuk asked.

"No, pretty close," said Griboyed, without turning his head. "Once we get through the burned-out stretch, we'll come to the pines and the road they built over the swamp."

"We're not going that way," Levchuk said.

"Wh—at? Which way, then?"

"Let's turn off here."

"How can we?" Griboyed demanded. "It's all swamp there."

"We'll cross it."

Griboyed considered this for a minute and then, with obvious reluctance, turned the horse off the road. But the animal did not want to plow through the dense undergrowth, so Griboyed had to climb down off the cart and lead the horse by the bridle. Levchuk also leaped to the ground, and, protecting his wounded arm with his good one, pushed ahead through the thickets.

He himself could not have said why, but he was determined not to take the brushwood road, even if seven scouts assured him it was safe. It had to be occupied by the Germans—he sensed it in his bones. Admittedly, he didn't know of any other road, and they would soon hit the swamp. He had no idea how to get across it with a horse and cart, but he consoled himself with the thought that he'd find a way when he got there. He had been schooled enough by war to know that many things became clear in time, on the spot, and that even the most farsighted plan—no matter how well arranged and thought out—wasn't worth much if circumstances gave the Germans an edge. During his life as a partisan, he had become accustomed to acting intuitively, never clinging blindly to a plan that might land him in hell's own amount of trouble, and let him drag others there too.

Griboyed let Levchuk know what he thought about this change in plans by shouting irritably at the horse as they pushed their way through the undergrowth, cursing the animal, pulling it by the bridle one minute, lashing its flanks with the whip the next. Levchuk began to get annoyed at the driver's show of resentment and was about to yell at him when the thickets ended and a broad water meadow opened up. The clouds had blown away and it was brighter all around; a cold mist hung low over the dewy grass, and there was a smell of rot and water plants in the air. Ahead lay the swamp.

The cart stopped, and Levchuk walked on

through the shallow grass until his boots began to squelch with water. Then he stopped and listened carefully. Firing could still be heard in the distance, but it was quiet here. Clumps of alder, their trunks submerged in the mist, were bent over the swamp. Somewhere a bird cried out faintly. The other birds must all be asleep. Levchuk walked on a bit farther, and the ground underfoot became softer—the moss had begun. He sank in up to his ankles, and his right boot, which had a hole in it, started to fill with water. But he still thought it would be possible to get through here—the horse would make it and the cart follow.

"Come ahead!" he called softly through the gray misty air.

He expected Griboyed to move and catch up with him right away. When a minute had passed and he heard nothing, he got angry. Apparently the driver had taken it upon himself to disobey Levchuk, who had been appointed his superior. After waiting a bit longer, Levchuk strode quickly back to the edge of the thickets. He found the cart exactly where he had left it. Griboyed stood beside the horse hunched over in his tight-fitting German uniform.

"What's with you?"

"Where're we going?"

"What do you mean, 'where'? Follow me! Drive along and follow where I walk."

"Into the swamp."

"What swamp? There's firm ground underneath."

"It's firm for a bit, but farther on it gets deep. I know that for sure."

Levchuk was ready to explode—he knew it was deep! They'd just have to get through that part, they couldn't stay here until daybreak! Was this the man's first day at war?

He knew it wasn't, knew that Griboyed was probably as experienced as anyone, and this kept Levchuk from flaring up at him. But he was simply amazed at the way the man went on muttering about the brushwood road.

"They told you to take the brushwood road. Isn't that what they said? But this is a swamp!"

"The road, you say. That's what you want?" Levchuk shot back. "How many times have you been under fire? Twice? Well, you'll get it a third time on that road, and it'll be your last! They'll do a good job of it!" Then, calming down a bit, he added, "Do you think the Germans are such fools that they've left the brushwood road open? Who cares what the chief said? You've got to use your own head."

Griboyed listened submissively and heaved a sigh.

"All right, I'm not arguing. Only how're we going to get through?"

"Follow me!"

The cart rolled slowly and noiselessly over the low grass to the edge of the swamp. The horse began to slip under more and more frequently: first a foreleg went down, then a hind, and in order to pull them out, the horse's other legs had to strain so hard that they too went under. The animal tried to jerk forward to find firmer ground, but there seemed to be less and less of it with every step. Klava climbed down off the cart and walked behind. Griboyed took the bridle and, stopping frequently, led the horse directly behind Levchuk.

But a time came when even Levchuk had to stop. Growths of sedge and the quagmire had begun, and pools of stagnant water gave off a faint gleam beneath the patchy mist that drifted over the swamp.

"Now we're in for it!" Griboyed said, and then he grew quiet beside the horse, which stood with its flanks heaving, clouds of steam rising from its body. Its hind legs were knee-deep in mire.

"Never mind, it's all right. Wait a bit and let the horse have a rest."

Levchuk tossed his jacket into the wagon and, gripping the stunted alder bushes with his sound arm, pushed resolutely on into the swamp. He no longer cared about keeping his legs dry. They were drenched up to the knees as it was, and water squelched in his boots. His wounded arm made the going harder, and he held it against his chest, his hand inside his shirt. Soon he sank in almost to his waist. But somehow he pulled himself out by an alder bush, where the ground seemed more solid. He'd have to figure out their next move from here.

"Come, this way!" he called.

The cart jerked, the horse plunged ahead—and sank in at once up to its belly. Levchuk thought as he looked back that the animal would pull itself out, but it didn't. It heaved from side to side, struggled, but couldn't get out of the hole. Levchuk, his boots gurgling in the slime, waded back to the cart and pushed from behind with his healthy shoulder, while Griboyed tugged on the bridle. Drenched up to the chest, Levchuk pushed for a minute with all his might and somehow the cart tilted a bit to one side and rose up out of the swamp. Klava moved on from behind, holding her skirt up over her knees when she came to the bad spot.

"Oh God!" she said.

"So much for that God of yours!" Levchuk retorted. "You'd better toughen up, you'll have to."

Again he went on ahead, feeling about in the water with his feet. But it was deep and unpredictable everywhere. There seemed to be no suitable way across this stretch. When he had gone about a hundred feet he still had not reached the bank. Everywhere he ran into mire, sedge, grassy tufts, and wide pools of black water with bluish haze drifting over them. He went back to the cart and grabbed hold of one shaft.

"Come on, heave!"

Griboyed pulled on the bridle and the horse, mustering all its strength, took one step and then another. The cart moved forward a little, but then stopped.

"Again, again!"

The two men harnessed themselves to the cart along with the horse, Levchuk pulling on the shaft, Griboyed on the bridle from the other side. The horse struggled and jerked, sinking deeper and deeper into the black mire it had churned up. It kept trying to move boldly ahead, exerting an almost supernatural effort to drag the cart, the wheels already axle-deep in mire. They were all up to their chests in water and slime, and sweat poured down Levchuk's face and back. Klava did what she could to push the cart from behind.

They went on struggling in this bad spot until nearly morning, and there was still no end to the swamp. Finally a time came when they all stopped and were silent. In order to keep from sinking into the mire, they had to hold onto the shafts and sides of the cart. The water was over the horse's back, and it arched its head high to breathe. If it hadn't had the cart behind, it probably would have started swimming.

For the first time Levchuk began to doubt the soundness of his choice and to regret that he had shoved on into this swamp. Perhaps it really would have been better to take the road—they might have slipped through. Perhaps they should abandon the cart and carry the paratrooper themselves? It was a good thing Klava hadn't started complaining. She had been bearing it all silently, and, to the extent she could, had even helped to push the cart.

"Now we're really stuck!" said Levchuk in despair.

"I told you so," Griboyed retorted. "Stuck like real fools. How're we going to get out?"

"Have we covered half a mile?" Klava called from behind. "Oh God! I can't stand any more of it!"

"We'll have to go back," Griboyed said. "Otherwise we'll drown the horse and this fellow too. And ourselves along with them. There're some really deep pools here, I tell you. Enough to drown you, and then some!"

Exasperated, Levchuk wiped his forehead on his sleeve and made no reply. He himself did not know what to do now, where to turn—forward, or back? And neither they nor the horse had much strength left; they were totally drained. *Perhaps,* he thought, *it really would be better to try getting through on the brushwood road.*

"Wait!" he said, panting for breath. "I'll have a look."

Again he pushed into the swamp, trying to splash as little as possible. In one place he fell into a pit and almost went under, but he managed to steady himself by clinging to a hummock. It proved to be a weak support, and he realized he couldn't hold on for long. So he plunged sharply to the side, toward some grassy tufts; there the water turned out to be shallower, and he started moving again, not across the swamp, but parallel to the shore. He was no longer interested in trying to cross the damned swamp, but only in keeping the horse, himself, and those entrusted to him from drowning.

The deepest part of all seemed to begin here. The water stretches became even wider, there were fewer hummocks and branches, and the alders had disappeared entirely. A boat would have been the thing here, not a horse and cart. Levchuk cursed himself again for his recklessness. *What a stupid mess I've made of things,* he thought anxiously. They would probably have to retrace their steps.

He made his way back toward the cart, which stood motionless in the swamp with the figures of Klava and Griboyed beside it. They were waiting patiently for him, but it would soon be morning, and that was no time to be caught in a swamp.

Suddenly a shot fired not too far away sent a resounding echo across the swamp. A moment later it was answered by a second shot, then by the shattering noise of machine-gun fire and the dull, heavy thud of a mortar. The mortar shell went singing high up into the sky and burst somewhere in the forest. This was the start of such a racket—thundering, screeching, and crashing sounds—that rent the otherwise still, misty night.

They all stood rooted to the spot. Levchuk, his mouth gaping open, stared into the night, trying to see or figure out what was going on, but in the semidarkness nothing was visible. Then he was startled into a triumphant realization. "It's on the brushwood road, yeah?" he called out.

"Yeah, the road," Griboyed answered gloomily.

Levchuk stood there, crushed by an awareness of the sudden disaster that had befallen the others, almost physically aware that it could have been their lot. They had escaped, but what was it like there for those under fire? Listening to the shooting, Levchuk couldn't help wondering who was winning. But then the answer was clear: it was the Germans who were winning—all the fire was coming from their side. And the sound of mortar fire was heard again—their own detachment had no mortars. Obviously, some of the men had counted on the scouts' reports, had been unable to resist trying to get through on the road, and were paying the price now.

Levchuk, shaking either from the cold or the sudden awareness of his lucky intuition, raced the rest of the way to the cart with a joyful fury.

"Damn it now, that shows you! And you wanted to go back? Come now, let's move! Give it all you've got! One, two—heave!"

Listening to the sounds of the firing, they again started pushing and pulling the cart, lashing and urging on the exhausted horse. But they had none of their former strength, and the cart had sunk in solidly.

After struggling for a while in vain, Levchuk straightened up. The firing on the road went on thundering in the distance, so he tried the swamp again, turning to the right and the left, feeling far out into the water. It was a good thing his boots were leather instead of the type with canvas tops. They had shrunk a bit and hugged his feet tightly. Otherwise, he would soon have been barefoot.

He decided that unless he went completely under, he would be able to get to the bank and think of a way to bring the cart out. Now he paid no attention to how deep it was, since he was up to his neck anyway, and he half walked, half swam, grabbing onto mounds of grass and dragging his body through the thick, stinking mire.

Strangely, the swamp no longer held any terror for Levchuk. On the contrary, the road was the place to be feared. The swamp had shielded him, saved him, and he even began to relish it. If only it didn't turn out to be endless.

Quite unexpectedly, he discerned the tops of shrubs through the mist; overjoyed, he realized that this was the shore.

Indeed, the swamp ended about twenty feet farther on. Beyond a narrow stretch of sedge, Levchuk glimpsed some alder bushes, and beyond them a meadow with freshly mown grass. Instead of steering his way to dry ground, however, he immediately turned back into the swamp and headed for the cart. This time he had trouble finding it and went farther in the mist than he should have, but he turned back after hearing a faint squelching sound. Klava was sitting in the half-submerged cart, trying to keep the paratrooper from getting drenched, while Griboyed held the horse still so that it wouldn't sink further into the swamp. Silently, they waited for Levchuk.

"Listen," he said, grabbing hold of one shaft. "We'll have to make it over one by one. Unharness the horse. We'll carry Tikhonov across on her, then maybe come back for the cart. The bank is close by."

4

It was beginning to get light when they finally made their way out of the swamp through a milky white fog. They had transported the unconscious Tikhonov on the wet back of the horse, Levchuk leading it by the bridle, Griboyed and Klava supporting the wounded man on either side.

When they reached the shore they barely had strength enough to lift the paratrooper off the horse's back. They laid him on the dewy grass and dropped down beside him. Levchuk lifted his left boot to drain out the mud; it flowed freely out of the right one because of the hole in it. Griboyed went about barefoot in summer, peasant-style, so he had no trouble with mud in his footwear. He took the bolt out of his rifle and blew into the mud-clogged barrel to clear it. Klava lay quietly, while the horse stood over them with its head bent low, the wet collar still on its neck, its flanks heaving feverishly.

"So! And you were against it!" Levchuk sighed with weary satisfaction. He caught the intermittent sounds of firing from the road with one ear, and trained the other on the deceptive stillness of the marshy bank. The most dangerous part began here—they could run into Germans at any turn. Cautiously glancing around him, Levchuk tried to prepare himself for any emergency. He pulled his Luger out of its sodden leather holster and wiped it on the hem of his jacket. The two cardboard packets holding the cartridges had gone limp in the water, and he discarded them on the grass, stuffing the cartridges into his pocket. Then he picked up Tikhonov's submachine gun. The paratrooper had been muttering something when they'd brought him out of the swamp, but he was silent now.

It was a pity there was only one magazine with the gun. Levchuk pulled it out and hefted it in his hand. It seemed full. He was about to remove the top in order to be sure, but changed his mind— he suddenly felt hellishly cold. His wet clothes were chilling him, and there was no way to get dry—

he would have to wait until the sun came up. The sky had already lightened, but there was still about half an hour to go to full sunrise.

Suddenly the wounded man began to stir on the cold, damp grass. "Water . . . water!"

"What? Water? One minute, brother, we'll get you some," Levchuk said. "Griboyed, go and see if there's a stream nearby."

Griboyed put the bolt back in his rifle and wandered off along the foggy shore. Levchuk shifted his gaze to Klava, who lay shivering quietly beside him. A momentary feeling of pity for her made him toss his damp jacket off his shoulder.

"Here, cover yourself."

Klava pulled the jacket around her and lay down again.

"Water!" the paratrooper cried out again, and he began to jerk as though something had scared him.

"Quiet, quiet. He'll bring you some in a minute," said Klava, raising Tikhonov up a little.

"Klava? Klava, where are we?"

"On the other side of the swamp. Lie still. . . ."

"Have we broken through?"

"Almost, don't worry."

"Where's Doctor Paikin?"

"Paikin?"

"What do you want him for?" Levchuk asked. "He's not here."

Tikhonov lapsed into silence. But then, as though he suspected something was wrong, he began nervously rummaging in the grass beside him.

"My gun! Where's my gun?"

"It's here. Where'd you think it was?"

The wounded man held out his hand demandingly. "Give it to me."

"Here, take it! But what do you think you're going to do with it?"

Clutching the weapon desperately, Tikhonov seemed relieved, though his relief had a noticeable tension in it. Next he asked in a husky voice, "Am I going to die?"

"Why should you?" asked Levchuk with deliberate gruffness. "You're going to live. We'll get you out."

"Where? Where're you taking me?"

"To a good place."

Tikhonov fell silent, evidently distracted, but then he thought of the doctor again.

"Get the doctor!"

"Who?"

"Doctor Paikin! Are you deaf? Klava!"

"The doctor isn't here, he's gone off somewhere," Klava told him, and she ran her hand down his arm soothingly.

The paratrooper licked his parched lips and began to speak in a trembling, agitated voice.

"But . . . but . . . I've got to know. I've gone

45

blind. . . . Wh—why? I don't want to live anymore!"

"Now, now, you're going to be all right," said Levchuk. "You'll want to live. Just hold on a little while longer."

"But I've got . . . to know . . ." The wounded man's voice broke off, and Levchuk and Klava exchanged glances.

"Tikhonov's had no luck," Klava said softly.

"Who's to say?" Levchuk replied. "The war's not over yet—we still don't know who's lucky and who's not."

Griboyed soon came back with his cap filled with water. But the paratrooper seemed to have lost consciousness again. Griboyed stood there indecisively with the water dripping out of the cap.

"Don't you have a mess tin?" asked Levchuk.

"No."

"Hey, grandpa, not too farsighted, are you?"

"I'm about as much a grandpa as you're a grandson. I'm only forty-five," Griboyed retorted, splashing the water onto the grass.

"You? Forty-five?"

"Are you really? And I thought you were at least sixty. Why do you look so old?" Klava asked.

"Because," Griboyed said evasively.

"That's life," Levchuk sighed, and he changed the subject. "We'd better try to find a village."

"Zalozye oughta be somewhere close by," Griboyed said, looking around. "If it hasn't been burned down yet."

"Let's go, then."

"What if it's . . . what if the Germans're there?"

If the Germans were there, of course, they'd better stay away. Probably one of them ought to scout around first, while the others waited in the bushes. If there was trouble—and there was likely to be almost anywhere—they'd have a hard time of it with a wounded man on their hands. But none of them had the patience to wait it out in this damp hole near the swamp. Thoroughly chilled, Klava was the first to get restive.

"Levchuk, we've got to go," she said insistently.

"All right! We'll go."

One by one they scrambled up, and then they hoisted Tikhonov onto the horse. He was still clutching the submachine gun, which they somehow managed to attach to the horse's collar. Feeling for the gun, Tikhonov put his arms around the horse's slimy neck and placed his yellow-bandaged head on its mane. Supporting him on both sides, they led the horse to the edge of the meadow. There was a little strip of woods, and there appeared to be a field beyond it.

They made their way around the open field, keeping close to the woods that bordered it. Now and then the famished horse bent down to snip bunches of the tall grass, and they had to wrestle to keep the wounded man from falling off its back. Griboyed angrily punched the animal in the side and swore at it.

"Watch it, you bitch! You can't eat here—"

"What's the matter with you?" Levchuk asked. "It's a living creature too—it wants to eat."

It was rapidly growing light. The mist that had drifted in from the swamp had almost cleared, and they could see far around them. The sky was a fiery purple—the sun was going to rise any minute now. In the early morning dampness it was bitterly cold; they shivered in the wet clothes that clung to their bodies, and their feet squelched and slipped in their sodden boots. Levchuk's shoulder was hurting him badly. Trying to move it as little as possible, he supported the paratrooper with his left hand and kept glancing from side to side, impatiently waiting for some indication of the village called Zalozye.

But judging by all the signs, they had ended up in a rather deserted place and would have a long trek to make before they reached a village. After the frantic struggle of the night before, they were hardly able to move their feet, and they walked slowly, fighting off the desire to sleep.

Now that they more or less had the swamp safely

behind them, Levchuk began to wonder about the outcome of the battle on the brushwood road. Had the partisans broken through? If not, it would be hot for them today. There were hordes of those German mop-up troops, and the detachment had been short of cartridges for some time. Most likely it had had no grenades left at all. On the whole, the commander had been right in making the decision to break out. . . . Who had he sent along the road? Perhaps the supply and medical units, which, of course, would have been wiped out. That's what it meant to rely on reconnaissance.

Levchuk had once served in reconnaissance and knew only too well what some of its reports were worth. After all, could you really find out all that much about the enemy on a patrol? Yet the commander always wanted things absolutely clear, so understandably quite a few guesses passed for the truth. . . .

Levchuk remembered how, as a scout, he had made a trip last year to the Kirov Brigade to pick up operators for the detachment's first radio set, which had been sent to them from Moscow. The news that they had gotten a radio had caused considerable excitement in the detachment—now they would be able to keep in touch directly with the main partisan headquarters in Moscow. The commander had called a meeting on the subject. Commissar Ilyashevich and some of the partisans had spoken, and they had all made promises and pledges about the responsibility they were undertaking with this equipment. . . .

Three of the best scouts were sent to pick up the radio operators, who were waiting some distance away. Levchuk was put in command—in those days he'd been one of the best scouts. Before they set out in the evening, the commissar and the chief of staff gave them lengthy instructions on what route to use, what equipment to take, how to talk to the radio operators, and what they should or should not tell them. Levchuk could not remember receiving such detailed instructions at any time before or after. It sounded like an extremely important assignment.

It was March, the winter was over, and the sun shone with increasing warmth during the day. By afternoon the ground thawed well, but late at night the road was like glass; the sledges scraped and clanged along, and the clatter of hoofs must have been audible for a long way. They covered thirty-seven miles in one night, and by morning reached the headquarters of the Kirov Brigade. There they met the radio operators.

The senior of the two was Sergeant Leshchev, a man no longer young; he looked sickly, had sallow skin and tobacco-stained teeth. They disliked him from the start. He kept asking them questions: where the detachment was located, how they were to get there, whether the sledges were comfortable and the horses rested, whether he could have something to cover himself with, since he was wearing calf boots with only one layer of foot cloths. They found a blanket for him and even wrapped his feet in straw, but he was still cold and complained about the dampness, the rotten climate, and certain of the partisans' rules that weren't to his liking.

On the other hand, the second radio operator, a girl, charmed them immediately. She looked so neat in her white fur jacket and her small felt boots, which made a pleasant crunching sound on the frosty ground. The earflaps of her beaver cap were tied behind her neck coquettishly, some locks of fair hair spilled onto her forehead, and her fur mittens were attached to the collar of her jacket with a white cord. Unlike the sergeant, she was delighted with everything, and laughed and clapped her hands with joy at things that intrigued her—a grove of birches, a woodpecker clinging to a fir tree. When she caught sight of a squirrel that had darted off the road, she stopped the sledge and chased it until her felt boots were soaked. Her dimpled cheeks became flushed like a child's from running, and her eyes radiated so much merriment that Levchuk gasped with admiration. He wracked his brain for some way to strike up a conversation with her, but couldn't think of anything to say. The others, too, seemed to have been struck dumb by her girlish charm, and kept puffing away on their cigarettes.

Finally, she couldn't help noticing their unnatural reserve, and, feigning bewilderment, coyly asked, "Why so silent, boys? Someone would think you weren't Russian."

It just so happened that she was right. None of them were. Zelenko was Ukrainian, and Levchuk and Mezhevich were Belorussian.

Just then, Zelenko, who couldn't speak a word of anything but Ukrainian, took it into his head to make a bad joke. "We—Germans!" he said.

And then Levchuk picked up on this and pulled an even sillier stunt—later, he was embarrassed to recall it. But who could have predicted what would happen? He was sitting in the back of one of the sledges when Zelenko came out with his remark, and he suddenly pulled open his sheepskin coat, revealing the warm German uniform he'd been wearing all winter. It had been taken from a prisoner of war, and was covered with braid and stripes. Levchuk shouted, *"Hände hoch!"* *

Before they knew what was happening, Sergeant Leshchev raced headlong from his sledge and took

* "Hands up!" in German.

cover in a ditch among a thick row of firs. The astonished Zelenko reined in the horse and they stared in silence at the firs, from which the shiny barrel of a submachine gun was pointing.

"Halt! Don't make a move!" roared Leshchev in a terrified, alien-sounding voice.

They hadn't yet figured out how to react when the girl let out a mischievous laugh. Falling back on the straw, she laughed so hard that her cap fell in the road and a pile of light, carefully trimmed hair tumbled out.

"Oh, it's too much! It's killing me!"

They succumbed to her mirth hesitantly, trying to smile, but at the same time they looked apprehensively at the firs. Finally, Leshchev cautiously emerged, but he did not lower his gun.

When the girl had laughed her fill, she picked up her cap and tucked her hair back under it.

"Okay, Leshchev. That'll do. You've given the partisans a laugh," she said.

Leshchev slowly lowered his gun and approached them, taking his place again on the back of the sledge; he seemed uncertain whether he had frightened himself and the others for no reason. There was an awkward silence, and Klava had trouble regaining her composure.

The next day, though, she was crying.

They had to bypass part of the Volkobrodsky

sector because some detachment there was fighting the *Polizei*.* And so they were obliged to stay overnight in a village where they had a connection. The man kindly took them in, heated the hut, and put some straw down for them to sleep on.

Before turning in, they arranged hours for standing guard, though their host had offered to act as sentry. (Levchuk didn't want to rely on him alone.) To be fair, they drew lots. Each of them had to do a stretch of two hours. Klava wanted to do her bit, and she drew a slip indicating from three to five—the coldest and sleepiest time of night. Levchuk, who was on guard until three, suggested that they exchange shifts, but she simply would not agree. He didn't persist, because he wanted to please her in every possible way.

After he had stood duty, Levchuk came into the hut shivering with cold. A wick lamp was flickering behind a glass, and the men lay snoring on the straw. Levchuk made his way to the stove in his freezing boots and softly called Klava. There was no reply, and he couldn't bring himself to try to wake her except by calling her. He simply didn't have the courage to touch the angular little shoulder under the field shirt. He called once more, but she went on sleeping sweetly, so he merely warmed his

* The *Polizei* were people in occupied areas who collaborated with the Germans and served as police. In German, the word literally means "police."

hands over the stove and went out again. He did another two hours' duty—for her—and then went to wake the men. They got ready for the rest of the journey.

When Klava awoke and realized what had happened she burst into tears.

She cried from feelings of self-reproach, from the shame of having slept through her first night of military duty, from the indulgence she had been shown. Throughout the next day she was silent and depressed, and Levchuk cursed himself for his timidity. But he had done only what he had thought best. He judged everything by his own partisan standards. How was he to know that this girl from Moscow might have her own yardstick? . . .

5

Beyond the woods lay a potato field, and there was no village in sight. They stopped the horse to look around. Freshly banked rows of potatoes with violet, starlike blossoms on their juicy tops stretched as far as the eye could see. They walked along the furrows in silence, stopping frequently to prop up Tikhonov, who kept threatening to slip off the horse. Although he groaned and his head was slumped over, Tikhonov kept a firm grip on the submachine gun strapped to the horse's collar. He seemed to be conscious, and, in fact, a moment later grunted through clenched teeth, "How much longer?"

"Longer?" Levchuk asked.

56

"How much longer do I have to go on suffering?"

"Not much, not much. Just hang on for a little while."

"Where are the Germans?"

"There are none here. What are you afraid of?"

"I'm not afraid. I just don't want to go on suffering for nothing."

Levchuk made no attempt to argue with him. He had seen plenty of wounded men and knew that badly wounded ones were sometimes like children, capricious and hard to please, and that you had to deal with them gently. True, sometimes you also had to get tough, though there were times when you simply didn't have the heart to.

Suddenly Klava cried out in alarm, "Levchuk! Levchuk! Look!"

Levchuk shot a glance around. The girl was crouching in a furrow, keeping her head down and looking off to her left. There, not more than five hundred yards away, were several tarpaulin-covered trucks parked, and figures in green uniforms were walking about between them. They were Germans.

It came to Levchuk with stunning clarity—they were trapped! Trapped beautifully! In the middle of a field, and with a horse! What were they going to do now?

It was too late to make a run for it. Griboyed dropped flat at once, concealing himself among the potato tops. Levchuk pulled the heavy body of the paratrooper down off the horse; unable to support him with one arm, he collapsed with him onto the field. Tikhonov began to groan, but then stretched out quietly in the furrow, while the horse, left to itself, stared into the distance in bewilderment.

"Now we're stuck. Really stuck. Worse even than the swamp!" Griboyed hissed.

Levchuk started to move closer to the horse, intending to pull the submachine gun off its collar, but the gun wasn't there. The paratrooper must have pulled it off with him as he fell. Levchuk looked cautiously out through the potato tops. The Germans didn't seem to be looking at the field, apparently hadn't noticed anything yet.

Perhaps they would soon drive off?

Levchuk held his breath in suspense as he lay among the dew-drenched potato leaves. The sun spread a broad fan of dazzling morning rays across the field. Perhaps the sun was blinding the Germans, so they couldn't see the strangers in the field?

The sun rose higher and the partisans went on lying there, not knowing what to hope or expect. Tikhonov kept quiet, though it seemed to Levchuk that he heard and understood everything that was going on.

Keeping watch through the leaves, Levchuk finally noticed that one of the Germans was staring into the field, looking in their direction. Griboyed must also have noticed this, for he began whispering fiercely to the horse, trying to drive it away: "Get going! Beat it, you bitch!"

But it was too late. The Germans must have spotted the horse, because a second man soon joined the first—a tall figure wearing a long coat and carrying a pail. The two men exchanged a few words, gesturing and gazing in the partisans' direction. Levchuk felt certain the Germans had not spotted them yet, that they had only noticed the horse.

Supposing they were to come after it?

The thought alarmed Levchuk, and he too began to hiss at the poor animal, which had still not dried off after its night in the swamp.

"Get the hell out of here! Beat it! Out!"

Unable to understand, the animal paid no attention to its masters' cries, and started plucking the potato leaves. Levchuk almost howled with irritation, but he couldn't get up to chase the horse away. He couldn't even give it a good slap.

"Griboyed! Drive it away! Get rid of it!" he hissed.

"Get going, you bitch! BEAT IT!" Griboyed tried to drive the horse away with a loud whisper, but it simply turned sideways in the furrow and calmly went on nibbling the young leaves.

"Drop dead! May the wolves eat you!"

It would have been a relief if the horse had died. But it obviously had no intention of doing so, and, once having started on the potato leaves, it hastened to get its fill. At his wits' end, Levchuk lay shivering in his furrow, glancing apprehensively at the Germans.

"Are the Germans far away?" Tikhonov asked. He began to stir nervously.

"Quiet! Lie still!" Levchuk hissed at him.

"Are the Germans far?"

"Quiet! They're right over there!"

"Are they coming this way?"

"No! Lie still!"

"They're coming!" cried Griboyed.

Levchuk poked his head out of the leaves for only a fraction of a second. But that was enough to convince him that the two Germans were striding slowly along the furrows. There was no question that they were headed for them. But the horse, still nibbling the leaves, had already moved off about twenty paces and might go even farther. A faint hope flashed through Levchuk's mind. The horse might be their salvation.

"Where are the Germans?" Tikhonov asked again anxiously.

"Quiet! Shut up!"

"*Where are the Germans?* Are they coming?"

"Yes, shh . . ."

"Are they coming to take us? They're not going to take me alive!"

His last words, which he almost shouted, struck Levchuk as a premonition of fresh disaster. He flung himself through the leaves at the wounded man, but just as he did there was a sudden burst of fire from the submachine gun.

Levchuk snatched the gun away from Tikhonov, thinking that he had been firing at the Germans. But then he saw the torn, bloody bandage on the man's drooping head, the blood streaming slowly onto the soft soil. He realized what had happened and jumped up, breaking the strap of the gun. Firing from the knee, without aiming, he sent a short burst of fire in the direction of the Germans, who at first halted, and then went rushing back toward the trucks. Griboyed's rifle cracked loudly, and Levchuk shouted, "Run!" Keeping their heads down, the three of them dashed headlong toward the woods.

"Oh, that fool! That idiot!" Levchuk swore as he ran. He had never expected anything like that, it amounted to treachery. The man hadn't considered others, had thought only of himself, of ensuring himself an easy death.

Levchuk soon overtook Klava. As they ran, they glanced back now and then at the trucks to which the Germans had fled. Several rifle shots rang out, sending bullets whistling overhead. But the woods were a considerable distance from the Germans and their trucks, and Levchuk soon began to feel more confident again, convinced that they could still make their escape.

Before diving for cover, Levchuk glanced around once again. Several Germans were standing near the trucks, following their movements. But they didn't take aim, apparently having lost hope of hitting the fleeing partisans. Some distance behind them in the field, the horse stood alone, flapping its tail. Tikhonov was no longer visible.

"Stupid idiot!" Levchuk blurted out, unable to control his rage. "All the trouble we went to for him, and he—"

One after another they darted into the woods. They kept on running, sometimes slowing to a walk, trying desperately to get as far as possible from that ill-fated potato field. The woods weren't thick; there were birch trees and patches of young firs. Levchuk, leading, avoided the denser places.

They could have run faster if Klava hadn't lagged behind, but Levchuk was afraid of losing her and slowed the pace. With great effort the girl caught up with them, grabbing hold of trunks and branches of trees to keep from falling. Levchuk could see that she was feeling sick, but this wasn't the place to stop. They had to move on as far as possible. He pushed stubbornly ahead.

After a while they emerged from the woods into a broad meadow where Levchuk allowed himself to stop to catch his breath and wait for Klava.

It seemed that the Germans weren't following them, but he was still trembling inwardly, and he felt that they had only escaped by a miracle.

Klava finally staggered out of the woods and dropped down on her knees in the grass; her face was blotched with brownish spots and expressed great suffering.

"Oh, I just can't go on! I can't!"

"What now?" Levchuk blurted out, unable to restrain himself. "We can't stop here! We haven't done more than half a mile."

"More like a mile," Griboyed corrected him.

"All right, a mile then! For them it's merely a couple of minutes. Didn't you see the trucks?"

They were all silent. Klava, still on her knees, fell forward on her hands, and, panting for breath, seemed on the verge of tears. The two men stood over her, not knowing what to do. Griboyed looked glumly at her from under his sheepskin cap, apparently suppressing some painful emotion—pity, or perhaps a feeling of guilt for all that had happened to her. Levchuk felt almost enraged with her because she was holding them up. This was simply no place for them—the Germans might overtake them any minute.

"Come, get up. We'll cross the meadow to that pine grove. There we can rest."

Klava took a deep breath and, visibly struggling to get a grip on herself, pulled herself up.

They crossed the meadow slowly, stopping frequently, and then Griboyed helped Klava across a stream. After they had climbed a low hill in the sparse pine wood, Klava collapsed in exhaustion on the dry heather. The men came to a halt. Levchuk took off his cap, which was drenched with sweat. The sun was high above them now, and he had warmed up. The day promised to be hot and still. They would have to get through it somehow, and in their position the hours till sunset were going to seem like an eternity.

"Well, so it goes," said Levchuk, looking closely at Griboyed. The older man stood there expectantly, breathing heavily and painfully in his tight-fitting uniform. "If only we could find a woman somewhere, or a camp with families."

"We need a horse and cart. How can we manage without a horse?" Griboyed asked reasonably.

"We had a cart, and a horse too. But like fools, we lost them. Now, look. You'd better go and try to find a village, grandpa. Maybe there's one fairly close by. But be sure there're no Germans."

Griboyed did not hesitate for long. He shot a worried glance at Klava and headed soundlessly down the hill.

"And don't be too long, hear?" Levchuk called after him.

Klava grew quiet, and Levchuk surveyed their surroundings. Beyond the pine grove there seemed to be an unplowed field, and then woods again— no sign at all of a nearby village. In the morning stillness birds fluttered freely in the branches of the pine trees; no shots or human voices could be heard. After scanning the grove, Levchuk walked around the steep side of the hill and listened intently. It appeared that there truly was no one around. He returned to Klava, and, still keeping his ear trained on the rustling sounds in the woods, sat down beside her. Convinced that Griboyed would not be back very soon, he pulled off his boots and spread his damp foot cloths on the grass to dry.

Klava lay on her side, looking at the grove with large, woeful eyes.

"I've caused you a lot of trouble. You must forgive me, Levchuk."

"We'll go into that when the war's over."

"Oh, if only we live that long."

"You must. He didn't, but you must. You've got to try."

"You think I'm not trying as it is?"

Suddenly she began to cry—softly, pathetically. He sat beside her, stretching his red, sore feet in the sun, and remained silent. He didn't try to comfort her, because he didn't know how to.

Klava went on sobbing for quite a while. Finally Levchuk couldn't take it anymore.

"Come on," he said, softening. "We'll make it somehow. Keep your chin up."

"Oh, I'm trying as hard as I can, but . . . You know what it's like."

"The main thing is to find some kind of shelter, but there doesn't seem to be anything around. I guess they've burned everything down."

"And the places they haven't burned are full of Germans," said Klava in a voice loaded with misery. Apparently this had been on her mind all along.

"Of course," Levchuk agreed grimly. He had

never expected such a turn of events. Only yesterday he had been at Dolgaya Gryada, wondering whether they would beat off the next attack, and, if not, how they would make their escape. And suddenly he had gotten this damned wound, which had changed everything, burdening him with the new responsibilities of Tikhonov and Klava. What would he do if her time suddenly came? He began to worry that it might happen right here, and glanced at her furtively. But after lying quietly for a while, she sat up on his padded jacket, leaning back on her hands. Her custom-made leather boots with their white, worn toes were wet from the grass, and the hem of her skirt was also damp.

"Take off your boots," said Levchuk. "Let them dry."

"Yes, but . . ."

"Take them off!" Then, realizing that it was hard for her in her condition, he stood up. "Here, let me."

With his left hand, he pulled off one boot and then the other. After a moment of embarrassment, Klava felt more at ease, and gave him a grateful look.

"How's your shoulder? Can I change the dressing?"

"It's nothing. Don't bother."

He had already grown used to the wound in his

shoulder, and regretted having gone to the medical unit. It would have been better to remain with his company. He might have broken through the German lines with the others, and never known the troubles that beset him now.

"What about Tikhonov? I don't even know what to make of it," he said, seating himself on the grass not far from Klava.

"He got frightened. Or perhaps . . ."

"He was frightened—that's for sure. But what would we have done if he hadn't been?"

"Maybe he did it for our sakes?" said Klava.

"Who knows? How can you even begin to figure it out? There's no way of telling what goes on in another man's mind."

"But you can tell a good man a mile away."

"Oh, can you! And you don't think the bad ones camouflage themselves? Like that swine? He seemed to be such a nice guy."

"Who?"

"You know who I mean."

After a moment of silence, Klava said, "Why talk about him now? We're all wise after the fact."

"Exactly—after! Wise and tough. But in the beginning we were so kind. While we stood there gaping, he put a knife in our backs."

"Platonov even said there was some suspicion. But there was no proof."

"Ah, so he was waiting for proof? Well, he got it."

They lapsed into a brief silence. Levchuk leaned back on his elbow and shot a glance around the pine grove. Then Klava began to speak softly.

"Naturally, we may have different opinions about Platonov now. You can blame him. But what was it like for him? He told me he thought something was fishy. But how was he to find out for sure? He needed time for that."

"He should have bumped him *or* them both off," Levchuk said simply. "What of it? Once there was any doubt, that bastard should have gotten it. So there'd be no doubt left. There was a case like that under Kislyakov. Some fellow came to us from a village and begged to be taken into the company. Yet his own brother was in the *Polizei.* So, what could we do? There was no way of knowing—he might have been honest, but he might have been an agent. So we finished him off. And everything was fine. At first our consciences bothered us, but after a while it passed. And I'll tell you—we didn't have any unpleasant surprises."

"No, you can't *be* like that," Klava said softly. "You've all grown so bitter in this war. It's understandable, but it's bad. Platonov wasn't that kind of man. He was humane. . . ."

"Ah, that's just it!" Levchuk retorted, and he

sat up straight. "Humane! Thanks to his humanity, what's going to happen to you now?"

"Well, I may be in for a hard time, but still and all he was a good man. Above all—a kind man. And kindness cannot be evil."

"What are you talking about?" Levchuk exclaimed. He jumped to his feet. "It can't? Now, look, supposing I'm kind and I soon dump you in a village, the first one that comes along. You want to find a place as soon as possible, don't you, so you can settle down and rest? So I arrange it. And the next day the Germans grab you. Or let's put it the other way around and say I'm not kind, I torture you and make you keep going, and you curse me. True? Still, maybe the place I'm dragging you to is much calmer, a place where you can give birth to your baby like a human being, where you'll have someone to look after you!"

He fired all this off in one breath, vehemently, and she remained silent. But Levchuk didn't care if she agreed with him or not—he was convinced of his own rightness. He had been fighting a long time, and knew that in war there was no other right.

Klava became absorbed in her own anxious thoughts. Levchuk walked barefoot over the prickly heather and looked down over the tops of the young pine trees to the grassy meadow. There seemed to be no roads or villages in that direction—but, blessedly, no sign of the Germans either. They were pretty well secluded here in this section of the woods, and it wouldn't be bad provided they could find a village of some sort. They simply had to find some place—a village, a farmstead, a forest ranger's hut—where there were people. Without help, Klava surely wouldn't be able to manage.

Levchuk went a little way down the slope, listened for a while, and then carefully walked back over the heather to Klava. She was lying on her side with her eyes closed, and he thought with amazement of how she had stuck up for Platonov. The man had made the girl pregnant and had gotten himself killed, but he still meant a great deal to her. Then again, she had loved him, so probably even the misery he had condemned her to had its sweet side. . . .

He sat down quietly on the grass and moved Tikhonov's submachine gun closer. He wanted to lie down and rest his exhausted body, but he was afraid he might fall asleep. So he sat there in the morning stillness thinking about their situation, about the poor wretch Tikhonov, and about where Griboyed might be wandering right now. Naturally, he couldn't help thinking about Klava too. She might have been right about Platonov. He had been a reasonable man, exceptionally fair with everyone, and calm in a decidedly unmilitary way. Levchuk had known him even before the war, when they had both served in Brest—Levchuk as commander of a signals section, and Captain Platonov as the regiment's assistant chief of staff for reconnaissance. Then the Germans had come, and, after the division had been surrounded and routed, Levchuk had spent the winter in the country at his father's place. In the spring, when their group joined up with Udartsev's, he met Platonov again. And it was simply amazing: the fighting, the defeat, the life they had been forced to live in the woods, in a forest full of both obvious and hidden dangers—all these seemed not to have altered the man's character. He was just as cheerful, steady, and consistent in his behavior with everyone, superiors and subordinates, as ever; and he never did anything reckless. He always tried to consider an action carefully before he made a decision. Only once had he behaved contrary to character by acting hastily, and that once it had cost him his life.

It had all started with the two Red Army soldiers who had appeared in the detachment toward the end of May. . . .

They had fled from the train station, where a large group of Russian prisoners of war had been unloading timber to be transported to Germany from the narrow-gauge railway line. They had asked

Zoika, the detachment's liaison at the railway barracks, to put them in touch with the partisans. And she had. By that time there were quite a few escaped prisoners in the detachment, so the appearance of two more aroused no suspicion. The suspicion and anxiety came a little later, when the special department started questioning the new men.

The first to be summoned was Shevstov, a tall man worn to a rail by backbreaking work, who said that he had been an engineer in Kemerovo before joining the army. He said that for a year he had been looking for a chance to escape and find the partisans. He was delighted that he had finally been able to, and asked to be given a gun so that he could fight those who had caused him so much grief.

It all sounded simple and ordinary, like the stories of many others in the detachment. Shevstov was recruited for the No. 2 Company without further hesitation, and sent across the stream to the company's shelter.

The interview with the other escaped man had to be postponed until evening, because Zenovich, the chief of the special department, had to get off somewhere, and the stableman had his horse already saddled near his dugout. Zenovich returned late, after the partisans had finished supper and were ready to turn in. He found the second escapee, whose name was Kudryavstev, waiting for him by his dugout. It turned out that the man had been waiting for about an hour because of some urgent matter he wanted to discuss with the chief. The story went that Zenovich was somewhat amazed, but that he handed the horse over to the stableman, opened the door of the dugout, and lighted the oil lamp on his desk.

Kudryavstev, an attractive fellow with black brows and an ingenuous smile, immediately offered a detailed account of himself: how he had lost his tank in heavy fighting, and how his comrades had saved him from burning to death. He even showed the chief a scar on his back, supposedly the result of a serious wound that had led to his capture. He said he had been born in Leningrad, and that before joining the army he had worked in a well-known factory; he also said he loved his country and hated the Germans, whom he was ready to fight in any capacity as a partisan, though he had been trained, among other things, as a first-class radio operator.

Kudryavstev also confided that not long before their escape, his partner, Shevstov, had been summoned to the chief of the German police office, and might have been recruited as an agent. Kudryavstev added that it was possible he was mistaken, since he himself had not been present at the talks, but he said that as a patriot and an honest man he felt bound to make the facts known to the detachment's command.

Zenovich spoke with deliberate calmness and told Kudryavstev he knew the whole story, though this was in fact the first he'd heard about the incident with the German police. He quickly brought the conversation to a close, and at once sent a guard for Shevstov.

Shevstov was asleep, and it was some time before he was brought in. On hearing the story of his having been summoned by the Germans, he expressed great surprise. Or, perhaps, he merely pretended to be surprised. He denied ever having been summoned, swore that he hadn't undertaken any obligations for the Germans and was not their agent. He had nothing to say against Kudryavstev—they had worked together and slept in the same barracks, and when they were carrying some old boards off the loading platform, they had seized the opportunity to escape.

Zenovich reported all this to the commander of the detachment, and, after discussing the situation, they gave orders to have Shevstov searched. When some of the partisans ripped open the seams of his trousers that night, they discovered a strip of cloth with some figures written on it in waterproof ink. When questioned, Shevstov was unable to come up with any explanation, and they all realized that it must be a German code. The partisans already had experience with this sort of thing, and the next day Shevstov was shot in a ravine.

Kudryavstev gained the general approval of the partisans for denouncing Shevstov. He had helped to expose a German agent, and in doing so might have saved the entire detachment; one could easily imagine what would have happened had Shevstov remained in it.

In general, the new partisan turned out to be a most likable fellow—he was a first-rate marksman, knew how to repair watches, and, in addition, played the accordion very well. True, the instrument they had was a mess, with torn bellows, keys that kept sticking, and notes that were out of tune. Yet Kudryavstev played so well on it that it was enjoyable to listen. When he had a free minute, he would take a seat on a tree stump beside No. 1 Company's bivouac and softly strike up "Suffering" or "A Modest Blue Kerchief." The men would gather around to listen, watching his fingers move deftly over the keys, and Kudryavstev would smile happily at them, quietly enjoying his own playing.

In time, Klava came to visit the No. 1 Company bivouac. She tried to make herself inconspicuous— she would come alone and stand shyly among the birch trees, behind the crowd of men, who would try to get her to move closer. Kudryavstev brightened whenever she appeared, and would go on playing with a smile intended only for her. Klava was a bit embarrassed at the attention she attracted, but she would stay on and listen, amiably fending off the advances of the bolder men who became a bit too eager. Actually, none of them was very aggressive, because they all knew something about her relationship with Platonov, the chief of staff.

Levchuk usually was present during the singing, or nearby, engaged on some small job. He was always aware of Klava's presence, and never let a step, glance, or smile of hers escape him. He immediately observed that Kudryavstev was attracted to her, too, and this put him on his guard.

Levchuk didn't know whether he himself was in love with Klava, or not. Perhaps he was just a bit fond of her, but he never showed it because he didn't want to stand in Platonov's way. From the very first glance she and the chief of staff exchanged on the day Levchuk brought her from the Kirov Brigade, he knew something would develop between them. They seemed made for each other. And so he gave her up, but only for Platonov's sake.

Klava began having trouble with her radio equipment, and one day she missed the morning exchange of messages because she could not tune in. By this time Sergeant Leshchev had been transferred to another detachment, but someone in staff headquarters recalled that Kudryavstev knew about radios. Kudryavstev gladly undertook to help; he tightened up one or two nuts and made some other adjustments, and the radio started to work again.

It turned out, however, that the radio didn't hold up for long; a gear wheel needed changing. But where in the forest were they to find one? After thinking it over, Kudryavstev said he'd try to get one from a man he knew at the German-held train station who'd trust him but no one else.

Platonov thought it over, decided to send Kudryavstev—not alone, but with a group commanded by Levchuk.

Levchuk had often gone to the station—he had some contacts there—and he didn't attach any great significance to the mission. He had been on much more difficult ones and had come through, so he saw no reason he shouldn't manage this time too.

He was due to leave for the station on a Sunday. On Saturday, while returning from Klestsy with a patrol of three other scouts under his command, Levchuk dropped in at a farmstead run by an acquaintance, who treated the group to some fine wine. When Levchuk finally returned to the detachment he was very drunk and the commander ordered that he be put in the punishment pit near the guardhouse dugout. Levchuk blew up and was rude to the commander, and was then obliged to hand over his submachine gun and march under escort to the pit. In a fury, he threw his jacket into the pit, jumped in after it, and immediately lay down to sleep, assuming he would be set free in the morning.

But he was not released the next morning or the next evening, and remained in the pit until Monday, when a rumor spread through the detachment that Platonov had been killed in an ambush at the train station.

When he heard this, Levchuk, unable to restrain himself, disregarded the sentry's shouts and jumped out of the pit. He dashed to the headquarters dugout where Klava lay sobbing and pounding the grass with her fists, and the commander of the detachment was raising hell.

Levchuk blamed himself for their chief of staff's sudden death. Because of Levchuk's arrest, Platonov had undertaken to head the group going to the station, and had set off Sunday evening with Kudryavstev and three other partisans. Two of the partisans were sitting before the commander now, describing what had happened.

Kudryavstev had betrayed him.

At first, things had gone well and there was no cause for alarm. They made their way to the station gardens in the dusk and hid in the dense hemp that had sprung up during the summer. When it grew dark, Kudryavstev set off down a narrow lane to see the man he knew, while the rest of them waited. They had to wait a long time, and began to think that something had happened to Kudryavstev. Finally Platonov lost patience and crept out of the hemp to see what was going on. But before he had had a chance to crawl under the fence, the partisans heard him utter a muffled cry, and shots rang out. Realizing that they had been ambushed, the scouts scattered in all directions. As they ran, they heard Kudryavstev shout to the *Polizei,* "Get that one, the one in the hat!"

The one in the hat was Platonov.

Later they learned that the chief of staff, wounded in the chest, had been taken to an interrogation room in police headquarters where he died, without regaining consciousness. After this, Kudryavstev disappeared from the area.

Klava was inconsolable. Levchuk gritted his teeth in grief and rage. A few days later he was transferred from the reconnaissance platoon to No. 3 Company as a regular machine gunner. And four months later he heard that Klava was carrying Platonov's child . . .

7

It was three hours or more before Griboyed returned.

Levchuk had moved into the shade. It was hot, and his foot cloths had become stiff in the sun. His boots had also dried up, and he could hardly get them on. Klava seemed to have a fever—she kept shivering. But Levchuk finally got her to relax and go to sleep. If she was asleep, he thought, *that* couldn't start.

He had a terrible desire to sleep himself, but wouldn't give in to it. To fight it off, he tried to keep busy. He took the magazine out of Tikhonov's submachine gun and removed the lid. The magazine wasn't full. He counted the cartridges. There were forty-three—enough for four good rounds. He reassembled the magazine, fixed the torn strap of the gun, and began impatiently looking around for Griboyed. He expected him to approach from the direction in which he'd left, but the older man appeared out of the pine grove, and the first thing he did was to shake the pine needles out of his shaggy hat.

"Well?" Levchuk asked.

"What can I say? Found a village out there, but it's been burned down."

"That's just great," muttered Levchuk. "We need one that's got people in it."

"Well, this one's been burned down," Griboyed repeated. "Only thing still standing is a threshing shed. From the edge of the village I thought it was empty, but then I saw a woman moving about there, near the rye field."

"A woman?"

"Yup."

"Did you speak to her?"

"No, I just spotted her and headed right back."

"All right! Well, then!" Levchuk said. "Come on, Klava. Get up! Is it far?"

"Not very. Over there behind the pine trees there's a ditch, and then a stream . . . and after that comes the rye field," Griboyed said, recalling the layout.

"Well, how far? Half a mile? A mile? Two?"

"Could be a bit over a mile, yes, or even close to two."

"Let's get going!"

Klava got up with difficulty and staggered, barely able to stand on her feet, and put her boots on.

Griboyed also looked exhausted and ought to have had a rest, but Levchuk was in a hurry to find people and escape from the feeling of being lost in the wilderness. His anxiety about Klava had mounted with each hour.

They walked down the pine-covered slope slowly, so as not to leave the girl behind, and then worked their way around beyond this. They soon came to a forest road. Before stepping onto it, Levchuk glanced to the right and the left and studied the tracks. They were all old ones—ruts washed down by rain, blurred imprints of hoofs and wheels. It seemed that nothing had passed by here in some time. Nevertheless, Levchuk swung the submachine gun off his shoulder so that he would have it ready, and stared at every turn in the road as he walked along.

"Why're you looking? There's no one here," said Griboyed. "I've already been here."

"What a daring fellow! He's been here!" Levchuk snapped back. "What if they're Germans here?"

"The hell with them. Fate'll decide. What can you do?"

"Listen, it's okay to think that way for yourself. But we want to live. Don't we, Klava?"

Stumbling along behind, Klava bit her parched lips and made no answer. Levchuk could see she was barely able to keep going. He knitted his brows anxiously. If only they could make it to this threshing shed Griboyed had found. Suppose *it* started to happen here in the woods, what would they do? . . . Griboyed's mention of fate was not to Levchuk's liking. He was against any kind of submissiveness, particularly in wartime, though it was easy enough to understand Griboyed's attitude. The man had had a hard life and had taken a terrible beating in the war.

"I'm not all that keen on living, you know. Don't really think I want to," Griboyed said now, scraping the caked mud with his bare feet. "What's life now that my family's all gone? What's gonna happen to me after the war's over? Who's gonna want me?"

"Come on!" Levchuk said. "You'll be honored when the war's over. Look at all the services you've rendered! Been in the partisans since the first summer, haven't you?"

"Yup, since the first."

"You'll be decorated, become a big man. Though to get a medal, you'll have to be more than just a driver."

"Phooey! What do I want with a medal? I want

my Volodka back. I'd give 'em all up, my girls and my wife, if only I could have Volodka."

"Was Volodka killed, then?" Levchuk asked, getting interested.

"Yes, practically in my own arms. Got hit in the side with a high-speed bullet. And all his guts spilled out. Such tiny little guts, like a bird's. I tried to push them back, tried. . . . But you know what a high-speed bullet can do."

There had been many horrors in the war, but Griboyed's fate had been particularly cruel. Levchuk had heard plenty in the detachment about the man's misfortunes.

Griboyed had lived with his family in Vyselki, a village set far back from the main roads. His farmstead was even further off—on the very outskirts of the village, almost at the edge of the forest. During the first summer of the war, the front rolled through the area almost unnoticed; by and large, the peasants were not aware of either the Soviets' retreat or the Nazis' advance. People went on doing the kind of work they had for hundreds of years.

On one particular day, the people of Vyselki were digging potatoes. Kalistrat Griboyed and his wife, aged mother, and older children were also digging. Shura and the smallest girl, Manechka, were warming themselves by a bonfire on the field divide where some potatoes were baking. Griboyed was in a hurry. He hadn't much more to dig when, at one point, Griboyed straightened up and caught sight of a man at the edge of the alder thickets. The man silently beckoned to him.

Griboyed tossed a potato into the basket and glanced around. His wife was busy raking the soil and hadn't noticed anything. Stepping across the furrows, he strode toward the edge of the field.

Hiding behind a small pine tree, the stranger waited for him. He was a Russian soldier, still quite young, who had been cut off from his detachment. He asked Griboyed for help, explaining that two of his comrades had been left not far away, on the other side of the swamp. They were wounded and couldn't walk. They needed a place to hide out in for a while. . . .

Griboyed took all this in and, without saying a word, went back to the field, harnessed his mare, and drove to the alder thickets. He brought all of the men back to his cottage.

For three weeks the wounded men—a colonel in the tank force, and a political organizer—lay up in Griboyed's cottage. Everything went well until the *Polizei* turned up. Griboyed became aware of the danger in time, and it was decided the Russian soldiers had better settle in the forest for the time being.

They built a dugout not far from Griboyed's

farmstead, and carefully covered it with fir branches and moss, camouflaging it so well that ten feet away you couldn't tell it was a dugout. They put an iron stove inside, heated the place up well, and, on the evening before the October holidays,* brought the wounded men over.

The men couldn't stay in the dugout for long periods at a time, and they had to be given food and clean clothing, so at night they would come over to Griboyed's. And frequently he went over to the dugout. Unfortunately, when the snow came, they began leaving tracks, which got deeper and deeper with the snow. They even formed a narrow path from the cottage to the dugout. Griboyed tried as hard as he could to conceal the tracks, but someone noticed them, and informed the *Polizei.*

Circumstances or, as Griboyed thought, fate saved him. The others were not so lucky.

Not long before New Year's they ran out of firewood, which they needed twice as much of now, because they heated the dugout frequently, and for long periods. (Despite this, it was cold, particularly for the wounded men.) There was no good firewood in the vicinity, and the peasants had to drive ten miles into dense forest to get any. One morning at daybreak Griboyed woke Volodka, his only son,

* The October holidays commemorate the Russian revolution of 1917.

harnessed his mare to a sledge, and drove off to a felling area for a load of wood. The felling area was a good distance away, but Griboyed intended to be back by nightfall, and to drop some firewood off at the dugout on his way home. There had been only a light snowfall since morning, so it would be safe—no tracks would be left.

But something unexpected happened. When they were crossing the Krivoy stream with their load, two of the struts in the sledge broke, and some of the legs pushed through into the snow and stuck firm. The mare pulled her hardest but couldn't get them up onto firm ground. They had to unload the sledge and make three trips to bring the wood up from the hollow. They didn't get back to Vyselki until almost midnight. Griboyed walked ahead, leading the mare, while Volodka, tired out, sat on the load.

They had about half a mile left to the dugout when shots broke through the still night air. There were only a few shots—several cracks from a rifle, a burst of submachine-gun fire—and then silence. It also sounded as if someone had screamed, but perhaps they had imagined it.

Griboyed turned off the road into a grove of fir trees and handed the reins to Volodka. Then he made his way through the woods to the dugout.

Before he even got there, he realized that there'd

been trouble. The door of the dugout had been torn off its homemade hinges, and the straw mattresses, bench, and other things from the dugout were lying in the snow, which had been trampled down by strangers' boots. The shooting must have taken place here, for the few cartridge cases that Griboyed picked up still smelled of powder.

Griboyed dashed through the snow and across the stream toward his farmstead, and could soon hear the *Polizei* barking out orders there. He heard the powerful voice of a commander and a woman's cry. They were looting his farmstead, arresting his family, and loading his belongings onto sledges.

He remained standing in the bushes until he saw three sledges set off for the village. He was about to run to his ravaged home, but when he saw the door hanging loose on its hinges, he remained stock still behind a pussy willow, holding his breath. He realized that all was lost, that only he and Volodka had survived. And the *Polizei* might have left some-one there to ambush him. . . .

He returned to the terrified Volodka, told him that only the two of them were left now, tossed the wood off the sledge, and drove the mare into the very depths of the forest. There they built a shelter out of fir branches; in it they shivered for two days and nights, eating the last of the bread they had taken with them when they had gone off for wood.

They soon began to suffer from hunger. That and anxiety for his family drove Griboyed back to Vyselki after another two days. This time there was no ambush. Griboyed walked through his freezing, unnaturally silent home, picked up some pieces of clothing and a bucket, and collected some potatoes in the cellar—that was all that was left, the *Polizei* had taken everything else. But these few remains of his property, together with the potatoes, saved Griboyed and his son during their early days in the forest. They built a small dugout in the thickets, and put together a stove that smoked terribly, but did give off a little heat.

The father and son might have lived well enough until spring if it had not been for their young mare, which also wanted to eat. No fodder was to be found anywhere in the forest in winter, but there was hay in the barn in Vyselki, and Griboyed, taking pity on the animal, made two trips to the farmstead. Everything went well—there was no shooting, and he left no tracks, because he chose days on which there was a snowstorm.

But one day Volodka begged to go along. Griboyed reluctantly agreed. He didn't want to take him, his heart ached with misgiving, yet when the boy climbed onto the front of the sledge, Griboyed didn't have the heart to send him back to the dug-out.

It was a rough, windy night. Branches of fir trees lashed out wildly, the snow whirled up in gusts, and the mare moved at a walk most of the way, turning her head away from the wind. By midnight they had gotten through the dense forest and turned onto the road leading to Vyselki. The farmstead was already close by, and Griboyed peered impatiently through the windy darkness. A wild hope came over him—that he would see a familiar light in the window of his cottage and find that his wife and daughters were at home, released by the *Polizei.* Because why should they be detained? What crime had they committed against the German authorities?

Griboyed did not know that his wife had been tortured to death in interrogations long ago, that his little girls had been taken away, and that his old mother, no longer able to bear the agony, had breathed her last in the cellar of the police station. And he did not know that for the third night in a row, three *Polizei* were lying in ambush at his farmstead.

And so Griboyed kept urging on his mare, drawing closer and closer to disaster. Already the bent willow near the gate, the well with its sweep, and the tethering pole near the barn that had been broken by strangers' horses were visible in the gloom. Suddenly the mare stopped, jerked her head up, and let out a soft, frightened whinny. He knew this habit of hers, a dog's rather than a horse's, and pulled on the reins. He stared for all he was worth at the dark farmstead. He could see nothing wrong, yet he sensed that something *was* wrong. Volodka whispered softly from behind, "Don't go there, Papa! Don't go!"

Hurriedly he began turning the mare. But before the animal could stamp out of the snow and bring the sledge around on the road, a fierce shout rang out from the yard. "Halt!" As Griboyed lashed the mare with the whip, a rifle shot cracked, and Volodka slumped over on the sledge and uttered something in a strange, altered voice. Griboyed paid no attention, but got up on his knees in the sledge and drove the mare for all she was worth. The horse broke into a gallop, and they covered the open stretch of road in a matter of seconds, with shots ringing out on all sides. Only when they had driven deep into the forest did Griboyed stop the sledge and grasp Volodka by the shoulders.

The boy was lying on his side and clutching his coat tightly over his stomach. His father broke his convulsive grip, pulled the coat open, and gasped with horror. Volodka's intestines, bubbling strangely under his hands, were creeping out of the bleeding wound. Whimpering quietly, the boy tried hysterically to push them under his bloodied shirt.

Griboyed brought him back to the dugout alive. Volodka murmured something in a faint voice, called for his mother, and then grew quiet. He lay silently until morning, only occasionally jerking an arm or a leg.

By daybreak he was completely still. . . .

8

Following the narrow forest road, Levchuk, Griboyed, and Klava climbed a small slope covered with pine trees, passed an old, overgrown felling area, and turned to the left. Fifteen minutes later Griboyed led them to the edge of a rolling field of rye. The patchy rye was ripening in several strips separated by carelessly made divides, and thick clusters of cornflowers and white daisies stuck up among the feeble stalks. Griboyed chose one of the wider divides and turned onto it; Levchuk and Klava followed behind.

"There's the little village," he said. "Or what's left of it, anyway."

Only from a few tall trees in the distance, beyond the rye field, could one have surmised that a village had recently existed here. No village was to be seen now, but as they drew closer they caught sight of the charred remains of stoves, overgrown with weeds; the partially burned corners of barns; and blackened beams lying about in the untended grass of what had once been yards. All that was left of many buildings were the foundation stones. The trees that had been closest to the fire had bare, withered, leafless branches. A tall lime tree over a well was green only on one side; the other side was charred, its black branches extending strangely skyward. Broken tubs and household utensils, sticks, and strips of gray rag were lying about in the trampled vegetable gardens. The village must have been burned down before the plowing had been done. No spring crops were visible anywhere, and the winter crop in the field belonged to no one.

"What have you brought us to?" asked Levchuk, stopping in horror.

"Come on, this way!"

Griboyed tramped quickly toward the edge of the village. They crossed a shallow ravine, and when they emerged from the bushes on the other side, they saw a small threshing shed consisting of two buildings that stood on a low hill near some alder thickets.

"See that? . . . The woman I saw was gathering something—roots or something of that sort."

"Okay, quiet now. Stay here a minute." Levchuk motioned Griboyed aside and walked quickly up the rise to the threshing shed.

A crooked path that must have been very muddy in spring began at the alder thickets and turned in the direction of the former village before reaching the threshing shed. There were no fresh marks on it, but Levchuk did not like the look of the path, and before crossing it he took a cautious look around.

Of the threshing shed's two buildings, the one closest to the path was a lean-to with the remains of last year's straw near it. Beyond it was the threshing shed itself, old and rickety, its beams and rafters sticking out like broken ribs from holes in the roof. Levchuk skirted a pile of stones at one end of the shed, and some dense patches of raspberry canes, and found himself on the side with the door. It was closed.

Seeing no one about, Levchuk quietly opened one half of the double swinging door. The shed was dark and smelled of dust and rotted straw; two swallows, squeaking faintly, raced by overhead. Probably they had a nest here. Levchuk opened the door wider and crossed the threshold.

Well, it looked as if Griboyed had not been mistaken when he'd mentioned a woman—someone had been living here.

On a pile of straw by the wall lay a piece of old sackcloth and some rags. There was also a worn sheepskin coat hung on the wall. A pair of leather boots with the tops cut down stood near the door on the cleanly swept earthen floor. Some light came in through the numerous cracks in the dark log walls. To the left of the entrance was a low door that probably led to the drying room. A rickety ladder was propped up against the wall near it.

Levchuk waited, listened a while, and then called out softly, "Hey, anyone here?"

No one replied; the place apparently was empty at the moment. *But whoever is living here will certainly show up sooner or later,* Levchuk thought, and he went outside. Griboyed and Klava were watching cautiously from the bushes.

"Come on!" He waved them over with his sound arm.

When they approached, he threw the door open with a welcoming gesture. Klava, who was limping so badly that she had to cling to the door to support herself, was the first to enter the shed. She shot a frightened glance around their grim shelter, and, catching sight of the sackcloth on the straw, immediately sank onto it.

"Well, here we are! And we're here to stay!"

said Levchuk. "But where's the owner, do you think?"

Instead of entering the shed, Griboyed walked on past the tangle of raspberries and nettles and stood listening. But all that could be heard through the gusts of morning wind was the rustling of leaves in a crab apple tree nearby, and the faint murmur of the swaying rye.

Levchuk climbed the ladder and glanced into the loft. He thought the inhabitants might be hiding here. But the loft contained nothing but a sprinkling of earth, untouched by human feet, and the droppings of swallows. The baby birds poked their heads from a gray nest under the rafters and emitted troubled peeps.

Levchuk climbed down again and opened the low door. Yes this was the drying room; there was a dense haze in the drying room, and the walls were blackened with smoke. A small window overhung with cobwebs cast only a gleam of light onto a blackened stone hearth that reeked of soot and mold.

"Can you hold out a little longer?" Levchuk asked Klava. But she did not reply. "We certainly could do with something to eat."

Unfortunately, they didn't have a crust of bread on them, and food was going to be a problem. Levchuk went outside and surveyed the rye field, and then a strip of potatoes caught his attention. The potato tops were full-grown, and there were some dry stalks lying in the outer furrows—that meant someone had already been digging there. Thinking that he too could dig some potatoes and boil them, he headed back to hunt for a bucket or basket to gather them up in.

"Hey, Griboyed! Let's have a dish of some sort. We've got potatoes here!" he shouted through the open door of the threshing shed.

But Griboyed remained silent, squatting on his haunches beside Klava, who, covered by the sackcloth, was bent over double on the straw. Levchuk gasped inwardly at the thought that *it* might have started. He stepped quietly over the threshold, but Griboyed waved him away, and he backed off without saying a word. *Poor Klava,* he thought. It seemed her time had already come, and there was no woman around to help her. And he himself would be no help. Perhaps Griboyed knew what to do?

Levchuk stood by the door for a while, waiting to see if Griboyed would say something, but he didn't. Then Levchuk remembered that in such cases the thing to do was to heat some water, so it would be well for him to get a fire going. He ran out to find some kindling, and turned up a few dry sticks. He broke them over his knee, and, working awkwardly with his left hand, managed to start a fire.

It was more difficult to find something to put the water in. But after searching for a bit, he found a battered pot among the raspberry canes. He plugged the hole in the bottom with a bit of wood, and ran down to the stream for water.

Levchuk kept listening for sounds from the threshing shed. Though he heard almost nothing, he didn't go back inside. He concentrated on tending his fire, which burned fairly well in the wind. The water was starting to get hot.

"That's the thing!" said Griboyed, dashing out of the shed. "You're a smart one!"

"How's it going?"

"Not bad. All right so far."

"Do you . . . you know something about this?"

"A little, yes," Griboyed said grabbing a rag that had been drying on a harrow propped against the wall. And he disappeared into the shed again.

So much the better, thought Levchuk. Maybe with Griboyed's help, she'd manage. It would have been worse if she'd been left alone with him. What could he have done? He tried not to think about what would happen if something went wrong.

Griboyed soon ran out of the shed and grabbed the pot off the fire with the grubby hem of his jacket.

"Already?"

"Yes, already!"

Levchuk was somewhat surprised—he had expected to hear a child's cry, or at least the groans of the mother. There had been no crying or moaning, yet this old midwife said it was all over.

"Come in one minute! ONE MINUTE!" Griboyed called from the shed.

Levchuk stood by the door feeling as agitated as a father who has just learned he has no further cause for agitation.

"Well, what is it?" he asked impatiently. "Boy or girl?"

"Boy!" Griboyed said in a voice that had taken on a new tenderness. "A fine little fellow. Come over and see."

With unexpected, almost unbelievable curiosity, Levchuk stepped into the shed and gazed at a bundle of parachute silk in Griboyed's arms. Beside Griboyed, in the dim light cast on the straw bed, Klava looked up at them with something like fear in her exhausted eyes.

"Look! Spittin' image of Platonov, right?" said Griboyed.

All you could tell was that the little wrinkled thing with its tightly closed eyes was a living creature, but to make the mother and her midwife feel good, Levchuk agreed.

"Absolutely."

"Now there are three of us men again," said Griboyed. "What're we going to feed on?"

Levchuk came to again. He, who had been feeling almost superfluous all this while, suddenly realized that he had some important responsibilities. Seizing the pot, he ran out of the shed and down to the potato field, where he started pulling up the plants.

Levchuk was filled with a new, thrilling sense of being involved in the age-old processes of human life. His feeling for Klava had changed completely in two minutes. She was no longer the flirtatious minx he had escorted to the detachment, or the girl who had disgraced herself by getting pregnant out of wedlock. Now she was a woman and a mother, and it was his responsibility to look after her. He knew only too well what it would be like for her as a mother in this wilderness, so full of the unexpected, and he was eager to make things a little easier for her. Strangely enough, it was thanks to Klava that for the first time in years Levchuk did not feel like a partisan fighter, a reconnaissance scout, or a machine gunner, but like a human being. It was an extremely pleasant feeling. It was as though the war had ended.

Slinging his gun over his shoulder, he set to work on the potatoes—washing them in the cold stream, filling the pot with water. He lugged the potatoes back to the shed, got the fire going again, and put the pot on.

"I've got a little salt," said Griboyed, when he came out of the shed and saw the potatoes cooking.

"Well! Maybe you've got some bread, too?" Levchuk replied.

"Nope, no bread. But I'll donate a little salt."

Griboyed knelt down by the fire, took a little red bundle out of his breast pocket, unwrapped it, then unwrapped some paper inside, and with two fingers took out a pinch of salt.

"More! What kind of a pinch is that?" said Levchuk.

"Must save some. Where're we going to get more?"

"How's Klava?"

"Fell asleep. She needs it, it'll do her good."

"And the little one?"

"He's sleeping too. Took a suck, and now he's sleeping. What more does he need?"

"Good. Sit, take a seat over here."

"No, I'll go in the shade. It's hot. I'm afraid my head'll start hurting."

The sun was broiling now, and it was hard to believe that they had been shivering a few hours back. But what did it matter—hot or cold? The important thing was that they had gotten away from the Germans and hidden themselves in this remote spot, and that there were fresh potatoes boiling away, promising their hungry bodies some satisfaction. The main danger had passed, and if it hadn't been for Tikhonov's death, Levchuk probably would have considered it a good day.

9

Levchuk had been sitting on the bench in the court-yard for two hours or more. The sun had gone behind the roof of the building next to Victor's, and the yard was bathed in a broad expanse of deepening shadow. No one had come up to him or bothered him; life in the courtyard had gone its usual way—the children amusing themselves according to their age, the adults busying them-selves with the kinds of little jobs people do on their days off. Some distance away, people were shak-ing rugs out and sweeping floor runners. There was also a young man beating a heavy, bright-colored carpet by the fence, striking powerful blows that resounded throughout the courtyard.

Levchuk had already studied every corner and path in the yard. On the whole, he liked the place— it was clean and well cared for. But there was so much noise, so many people around—it was like a marketplace on a holiday. Of course, it was all a question of what you were accustomed to. He, for example, had grown used to the quiet of the country, which was disturbed less often by the voices of people than by the sounds of animals and birds, or the distant chugging of a tractor in the field. Here there was noise and bustling and chatter all the time.

As he sorted out his memories of those terrible days in the summer of 1943, Levchuk couldn't help asking himself, *What is he like now?* Sometimes Levchuk would picture Victor as a tall man with a self-confident expression and an attentive smile. Levchuk did not like taciturn people. He was none too talkative himself, but Victor must be better than Levchuk in all respects. He might be an engineer or a specialist in machine parts or mechanisms— there were many of them around these days. Perhaps he even designed cars. Levchuk had acquired a liking for cars long ago, and if it hadn't been for his arm, he would have liked to become a driver. But with one arm it was hard—you couldn't accomplish that much. . . .

Then again, perhaps Victor was a doctor in some well-known hospital where he performed operations and treated people. Levchuk knew how important this was, having been in hospitals many times since the war.

10

The potatoes were boiling, and to be sure they wouldn't overcook, Levchuk jabbed at them with the cleaning stick he had removed from the butt of the submachine gun. The potatoes were still hard, however, and he threw everything he could find on the fire—bits of stick, a board, some of the straw heaped near the lean-to. Griboyed sat in the shade near the wall of the shed and watched him.

After a few minutes, Levchuk poked into the pot again. This time he felt the cleaning stick go through the potatoes and touch bottom. He asked Griboyed to drain off the water—it was hard for him to do it with one hand. Griboyed covered the pot with the hem of his woolen jacket, and tipped it to one side over the grass. There wasn't much water left. He waited for the last drops to drain out, and then put the pot back on the fire.

"Let them dry a bit."

"What for? Take them inside, we're going to eat."

Griboyed picked up the steaming pot again, and Levchuk opened the door of the shed. Cradling the little white bundle in her arms, Klava was beginning to doze, but she woke at the sound of the door, and Levchuk thought he detected a faint smile on her lips.

"Come on, let's eat! Here're some fresh potatoes. Bet you haven't eaten anything fresher this year."

She made an attempt to raise herself and Levchuk helped, propping some straw behind her back. Holding the baby in her arms, she somehow managed to make herself comfortable and to push the hair off her forehead.

"Is he asleep?" Griboyed asked, moving the pot over to her.

"Yes."

"That's good."

"It's all right, let him. Means he'll grow up to be a calm man like his dad," said Griboyed.

"Thank you," said Klava humbly.

"Nothing to thank me for. . . . A woman would have managed better, of course."

110

"You didn't do so bad!" said Levchuk. "Not a cry, not even a whimper!"

"Had nothin' to do with me. What'd I do? It was her that did it."

Scorching their fingers, Levchuk and Griboyed began pulling the hot potatoes out of the pot. Klava sat quietly against the wall with the little one nestling in her arms. Glancing at her, Levchuk said, "Come on now, eat. You've got to keep your strength up."

"There was a spoon in my bag," she said.

Levchuk pulled her light German field bag out from under her and rummaged through it.

"Here it is."

"And there's a little flask. Get that out too— for the occasion."

"A flask? Oho!" Levchuk roared. He quickly withdrew an aluminum flask with liquid faintly splashing inside. "Home brew?"

"A little spirits. I'd been saving it."

"Good for you, little mother!" Levchuk said enthusiastically. "God give you health, and the little one too. Griboyed, going to have a drop with me?"

"Suppose so, seein' it's such an occasion," Griboyed replied shyly, his eyes sparkling with good humor.

Eagerly and with a certain solemnity, Levchuk took a drink of the spirits. He gulped, gasped, waited a second, and then bit into a potato with relish. He passed the flask to Griboyed, who frowned, took a small swallow, and then frowned even more, wrinkling up his entire face.

"Yech! Home brew's better."

"No comparison! This is pure spirit, from a factory, while home brew—"

"What do I care if it's from a factory? I say the other's better, goes down easier."

"Aren't you going to have a drink?" Levchuk asked Klava.

"I don't think I should," she said shyly.

"Why not?" said Griboyed. "Drink up. When my wife was feeding her baby, she'd have a drink sometimes. On holidays. Makes the baby sleep good."

"Well, just a little . . ."

She brought the flask to her lips and took a sip. Levchuk grunted with satisfaction—he was as receptive now to another person's pleasure as if it were his own.

"Well now, that's fine! Here, eat up. Even though the potatoes aren't peeled, they're tasty, right?"

Klava ate one and said, "Yes, they're very good potatoes. I don't think I've eaten any this good in my life."

"Like mushrooms! If only there was a bit more salt. Eh, Griboyed?" he hinted. But Griboyed merely turned his head.

"No, I'm not givin' any more. There's only a little bit left. We'll be needin' it."

"I didn't know you were so stingy."

"Am I? It'd be different if there was a lot, but there's only enough for a lick."

Klava ate two more of the potatoes and leaned back against the wall.

"Oh, my head is swimming!" she said.

"It's nothing, it'll pass," Levchuk said reassuringly. "Ah, I feel so good—as if a band was playing in my head."

Griboyed looked at him disapprovingly. The lines in his face seemed more deeply etched than usual.

"What's there to be cheerful about? Look where the sun's still at."

"What of it?"

"Long time till evening."

Like the other two, Levchuk had tired himself out during the night, and he had gotten a bit tipsy from one drink on an empty stomach. He felt strong and confident. Naturally, he knew that all sorts of things could happen, but he had a submachine gun and one strong arm, and he'd learned how to use the other one to help, and how to ignore the pain. During the war he'd been in dozens of the most improbable situations, and so far he had always come out alive. Besides, it seemed unlikely that anything bad could happen in this quiet spot.

The others didn't seem quite so positive.

Griboyed became noticeably more pensive and troubled. While he was munching on a potato, his jaws suddenly stopped working and he stared ahead with a fixed look. Klava managed to do everything at once—to eat and to attend to the baby in a nervous sort of way, and at the same time to listen for something outside. When Levchuk had noticed her doing this, for the fourth or fifth time, he asked, "Why do you keep pricking up your ears?"

"Do I? I think I can hear something—like voices."

They all listened intently but heard nothing. Levchuk picked up the submachine gun and went outside to double-check.

It was nearly high noon, and the sun was beating down on the roof of the shed. The leaves of the crab apple tree rustled faintly, but otherwise a drowsy silence pervaded the heat-drenched fields. There was no one to be seen anywhere. Levchuk walked around the shed once and then went back in.

"You're imagining things, Klava. There's no one there."

"Perhaps I am," Klava said, reassured. "I get that way sometimes. When I was a little girl I was such a coward! I was afraid to stay at home alone, particularly at night. We lived on Solyanka Street in Moscow, in an old house, and there were loads

114

of mice. My father was often away on business trips, and when Mama came home late I'd be hiding behind the sideboard and crying. I was afraid of the mice."

"Mice?" Griboyed asked in amazement.

"Yes."

"Why be afraid of mice? You think they bite?"

"Mice are okay. But you take wolves. Wolves are another thing entirely. I'm afraid of wolves, they gave me a real scare once," Levchuk said, stretching out with pleasure on the firm earthen floor. "I could do with a nap. What do you think, Griboyed?"

"You know best, you're in charge."

Griboyed ate the last of the potatoes, though with no real zest. Levchuk yawned once, then again, and wondered how to arrange things so that Griboyed would stand guard for a couple of hours while he got some sleep. He was fiendishly exhausted, particularly now that he had had a drop to drink and appeased his hunger. But before he could say anything to Griboyed, Klava let out a sob and burst into a fit of uncontrollable crying. Levchuk jumped up.

"What's going on? What's wrong? Come on, what is it? Everything's all right, Klava!"

But she went on sobbing, with her shoulders shaking and her face buried in her hands. Levchuk couldn't understand what had happened and tried to reassure her. Griboyed sat quietly with his bare feet tucked under him and watched the two of them sadly.

"Leave her be," he said to Levchuk after a while. "Let her cry. Everyone has something to cry about. So has she. Leave her alone."

Levchuk went back to his place, and Klava, after letting out a few more sobs, wiped her eyes on the sleeve of her field shirt.

"I'm sorry, I just couldn't stop. I won't do it again."

"No more jokes from you," Levchuk said seriously. "Or we'll start howling just looking at you."

Her lips twitched and it looked as if she was going to break down again. Griboyed hastened to reassure her.

"It's nothing. Everything's going to be all right. The main thing is you have your child, a fine boy. He'll grow up, and when this damned war ends, everything will be all right. It'll be fine for the young ones. An old man's got nothing to look forward to, but the young ones'll have their whole lives in front of them. Don't get yourself upset."

The baby got restive in his mother's arms. He began to fuss in his silk bundle and, for the first time, raised his tiny, weepy voice. Klava rocked him very carefully but somewhat unskillfully, saying something tender to it over and over again in a soft voice.

"Hey, he probably wants to eat."

Levchuk turned away while Klava took the child to her breast, pulling the sacking around her.

Levchuk relaxed and stretched out on the floor. "If it hadn't been for the war," he said, "I'd have had a wife. Had my eye on one. Ganka was her name. But there wasn't any Ganka, any wife in store for me. Just the war."

"Good heavens!" said Klava, her voice full of anguish. "What did I know about war? I asked to go, volunteered. They didn't want to take me, and I had to use pull to get into radio school. I thought . . . And then this! Lord, all the grief, blood, death! How do the local people stand it? The men do, that's understandable. But the women, girls, little children! Why are those poor creatures tortured so? Beaten, hunted down with dogs, burned! And with such savage cruelty!"

"They're defenseless, that's why," Griboyed said with a heavy sigh. "Defenseless."

"God!" said Klava. "Up till now I just had to worry about myself, but now I have to be doubly scared—for him. So tiny! My poor little darling, my poor little boy, how am I going to take care of you?"

"Enough of that wailing!" said Levchuk. "We'll

nurse him through somehow. The thing is to find the right place."

"But it's too soon to start movin'. She needs to rest a bit," remarked Griboyed.

"Let her. You stay with her. I'll get going. We've got to find some people. There must be *someone* around. The Germans can't have killed all of them."

"You oughta go to Kruglyanka. It was still standin', last I knew. It must be about six miles from here."

"Right, I'll go there. I used to know a man there. He rounded up some of the *Polizei* with us in May."

"Or you could try Shipshinovichi, 'cept I'm not sure if it's still there. It's in the forest—or was."

"I doubt if it is, then. Give me the pot and I'll go for water. I'm thirsty."

Just as Griboyed reached out to hand the pot to Levchuk, Klava shuddered with a sense of foreboding.

"What's up?" Levchuk asked in bewilderment.

"Do you hear?"

"What?" Levchuk snapped. But before he could get halfway across the shed, he froze.

From somewhere in the noonday stillness, they could hear a harmonica playing. Without a word, Levchuk grabbed his submachine gun and raced for the door.

11

Levchuk opened the door just a crack, and then closed it immediately. Through the narrow gaps between the boards he spotted two carts with dark-uniformed figures in them coming down the road. The figures wore black caps, and had rifles in their hands or over their shoulders. There were the sounds of voices and laughter, in addition to the soft tones of the harmonica.

Levchuk swore.

"Who's there?" Klava cried out in fright. "Is it the Germans?"

"Just as bad—the *Polizei*," said Levchuk, and he stepped back from the door. "Griboyed—into

119

that corner!" He sprang over to Klava and pulled the sheepskin coat from behind her back. "Lie down! And be quiet! They're driving past," he said, though he hardly believed his own words.

Griboyed obediently darted for the corner, found a convenient slot to look through, and kept his eyes glued on the road. Levchuk raced back to the crack near the door and fixed his attention on the carts, which rolled quickly downhill to the stream, crossed it, and slowed down for the climb toward the shed. He counted the riders—there were four in the first cart and three in the second. Everything hinged on whether they drove past or stopped near the shed.

No, they were not going past. The carts came to a halt on the near side of the stream. There was a shouted command, someone jumped down off a cart, and then they all got down. Levchuk's heart contracted with foreboding. It didn't look as if they'd get out of this one easily.

"Griboyed! Keep an eye on them! And keep quiet!"

It was quiet in the shed without his orders. Instead of covering herself with the sheepskin coat, Klava knelt on the straw and, clutching the baby to her, watched Levchuk's every move. Griboyed crouched tensely beside the crack in the wall.

What are they going to do? What are they going

to do? Levchuk kept asking himself as he watched them sort out weapons and stuff cartridge clips into their pockets.

Then, leaving the carts on the road, the *Polizei* moved up the path leading to the shed. As they did, they broke into two groups. One headed directly for the shed, while the other, smaller group made its way toward the alder bushes.

It would all have been simple and clear if they hadn't behaved so casually. But it was as though they didn't suspect a thing. They smoked and chattered as they walked openly along the path leading to the shed, showing no sense of danger. It was precisely this affected casualness that threw Levchuk off and led him to think they might just walk on past the shed. Numb with suspense, he pressed close to the wall and cocked his gun, with his left thumb to make sure the weapon was set for firing in rounds.

The group of four was walking toward the threshing shed at a carefree, relaxed pace. Levchuk could easily have cut them down with one well-aimed burst, but the vagueness of their intentions kept him from doing so. Supposing that for some reason they did go on past, to the rye field? *How could they possibly know there are partisans in this shed?* thought Levchuk.

"Levchuk! What's going on? Where are they?"

Klava whispered in despair. But he merely shook his head.

"Quiet!"

For a few minutes the four men were hidden around the corner of the shed. Levchuk pressed his forehead against the rough log wall, but couldn't see anything. Then the *Polizei* appeared right next to the wall, just beyond the raspberry canes. First came a burly man whose belt sagged under the weight of his heavy cartridge cases. He was carrying a German rifle in one hand and a cigarette in the other; he took a few quick drags on the cigarette before tossing it on the ground. Now he had reached the middle of the yard, but Levchuk still had a faint hope that he would move on past. Through the crack, he followed the direction of the man's glance, which strayed first along the side of the shed, pausing briefly at the dense patch of raspberry canes at the corner, and then swept around and focused on the remains of their fire. A barely visible wisp of smoke rose from the embers. Levchuk cursed himself inwardly for his fateful carelessness.

The *Polizist* walked over to the door, and it swayed with a faint creak.

With his back to the wall, Levchuk held his gun ready, still unable to relinquish all hope. He knew that from the outside not much was visible in the darkness of the shed. But before the man had a chance to fling the door open, Klava made a dash across the floor, and three shots rang out. The man let out a little cry and disappeared from view. Levchuk aimed a short burst of fire out the door, and, sensing that it would soon be returned, stretched out on the floor. Klava crouched against the wall, trembling with fear, a pistol in her hands.

"Lie down! Lie down!" Levchuk managed to shout before the first bullet from outside hit the wall. It knocked a thick wedge from one of the logs near the door. Shots rang out on both sides of the shed at once, and in several places bullets smashed through the rotting log walls, scattering mold and dust on the clay floor.

Levchuk did not remain at the door for long, but crawled quickly to the wall opposite it and peered through a crack near the floor. Bullets thundered overhead and came in under the roof, but the foundation stones gave them some cover close to the ground. The raspberry canes growing around the shed screened the cracks completely in some places, and Levchuk feared that the bastards might come too close without his seeing them. At close range they could rush the door and toss in a hand grenade, or simply gun them down point-blank. The thing to do was to keep them as far from the shed as possible, make them shoot from a distance.

Now that the fighting had begun, Levchuk's uncertainty had disappeared completely because his naïve hope was gone. He realized that they had gotten themselves in a fix, a really bad fix, but everything in him was geared to one aim—not to surrender.

He dashed from one wall to the next, peering through the cracks, but the *Polizei* seemed to have ducked for cover, and until Griboyed began firing from his corner, Levchuk could not figure out where their attackers were.

Klava lay by the wall, pressing the baby close to her, not taking her eyes off the door. Levchuk merely had to glimpse the desperation in her eyes to realize how rough it was for her. He wanted to say something encouraging but couldn't find the words, and, cursing silently, he dashed into the drying room. He had to try to cover them on that side.

It was almost dark in the sooty-smelling room; the only light came in through the narrow little window. Levchuk thrust the barrel of his submachine gun through the murky glass and immediately flattened out on the floor. A shot rang out at once from not far away. With a sinking heart Levchuk realized that they were covering this side of the shed too, and that there'd be no chance of making a break for it through the rye. Their position was getting worse by the minute.

After lying still for a while, he cautiously raised himself to the little window and glanced to the side, in the direction of the alder thickets. Two dark figures in field caps were standing up to their chests in the rye, guarding the edge of the field. Levchuk fired a quick burst in their direction to let them know there was someone guarding this spot. Then he bent low, stepped back over the high threshold of the drying room, and flopped down near Griboyed, who was still keeping a close watch through his crack in the wall. Klava was now lying behind a stack of straw, using her own body as a shield for the baby.

A single shot rang out and a bullet whined overhead. Then, for some reason, the shooting suddenly stopped.

"Griboyed, do you have many cartridges?" Levchuk asked in a low voice.

The older man rolled over on his side without taking his eyes off the crack, felt in the pockets of his uniform, and pulled out a few clips.

"Four clips."

"That's all?"

"Yes."

"And you, Klava?"

"I had eight bullets."

"You've fired three, so that leaves five. God, what a way to fight!"

It was a rotten, if not a hopeless, position to be in. They were surrounded on all sides and could be kept under constant fire. The *Polizei* had plenty of cartridges, of course, and it was absurd to think that they could hold them off for long with a mere fifty or so. But if they didn't? . . .

Lying still, Levchuk set his submachine gun for single firing. From now on he would fire only carefully aimed shots, one at a time.

"What are we going to do, Levchuk? Oh, God, what?" Klava asked in quiet desperation.

"Quiet! Stay down! Keep your eyes on the door. If anyone comes in, shoot straight for his head!" He looked at the door, dreadful to him now, a huge door made of thin unplaned boards, consisting of two panels that opened outward. There was no way to buttress it or keep it shut. The bastards had only to hurl one hand grenade and there would be no door left at all. . . .

The lull in the firing continued for a while. Probably the *Polizei* were discussing what to do. And then a voice reached them from somewhere not too far off.

"Hey, Mophead, don't you think it's time you gave up?"

Levchuk shuddered. In Reconnaissance, he'd once had the nickname "Mophead"; and that voice sounded so familiar . . .

"Hey! Can you hear me? Better give up before we set fire to you. Or are you done for already?"

"It's that one," whispered Griboyed, turning to Levchuk. "The one that came to us from the station."

"Kudryavstev?"

"Yes!"

Levchuk swore quietly. He was astounded by the discovery. He lay silently for a minute, aware of an overwhelming desire to dash out of the shed and pump every bullet he had into that scoundrel. Let them kill him if they wanted to after that. But he managed to squelch his anger and, instead of dashing out, he crawled closer to Griboyed.

"Over there on the other side of the lean-to," said Griboyed. "He's poking his head out from behind the straw."

"Give that to me!" Levchuk said. He took Griboyed's battered old rifle and settled in better along the wall. He tried as hard as he could to shove the rifle into the crack, but only the very tip with the front sight fit. It was a good thing the raspberry canes hid the cracks from the outside. But the view from within was bad, and Levchuk had trouble aiming the rifle at the spot where Kudryavstev was lying in the straw. He waited for him to move, and after the top of his black field cap came into view, he fired. Then, quickly reloading the rifle, he shot at the same place again and waited.

But he didn't have to wait long. As though nothing had happened, the loud familiar voice rang out again.

"You'll finish yourself with your shooting, Mophead!"

"You're the one who'll get it!" Levchuk roared back.

"Stop fooling around, you idiot! Send the radio operator out and put your hands up! We'll spare you!"

"I'll make it without your help, you bastard!"

"You'll be sorry!" Kudryavstev yelled. "Okay, men, fire!"

This time they fired a volley the like of which Levchuk hadn't heard in some time. Shots thundered from the lean-to, from along the road, from the alder thickets; it sounded as if an entire platoon was blazing away at them from all four sides. The bullets drilled and fractured the rotten wood of the walls, sending mildew and splinters down on their heads; the dust rose to the rafters. If the raspberry canes hadn't shielded the foundation, which continued to save them from the bullets, they probably would all have been killed. It was impossible for them to raise their heads and look through the cracks, but someone had to be on the watch.

Levchuk knew there was a motive behind this

kind of shooting, that under its cover these wolves would try to get closer to the shed. As he lay by the wall he listened closely to the frequent, irregular shots, trying to determine when he'd have to shoot back. He'd had some experience with this kind of thing, and he felt rather than saw when the *Polizei* were close. He picked up his submachine gun and fired through a crack—first in one direction, then in another. Nearby, Griboyed's rifle thundered several times.

Keeping his head low, Levchuk saw through the raspberry canes that one man had fallen and that another, his head down, had darted for the lean-to. The *Polizei* weren't interested in getting killed here. A minute later shots rang out again from the alder thickets, but there was no sound from the lean-to. Just when it looked as if they had won another breathing space, Levchuk was seized by a new fear. He dashed to the end of the shed and raced up the ladder to the loft.

He took three steps in the soft earth scattered there and flung himself down on an old straw screen. It had several holes in it, and through one he looked down on the rye field, gloating with revenge. Two men with black field caps were creeping furtively toward the shed. Levchuk slowly cocked his gun. The *Polizei* were crouching in the rye for cover and could not see him. He took careful aim and fired a single shot. The nearer of the *Polizei* seemed to leap up in surprise, but then he threw back his head, spun around on his heels, and crashed head-long into the rye. The second dashed into the alders. Levchuk fired hastily after him, knowing full well he couldn't hit him, and immediately regretted wasting the cartridge.

Two shots were enough for them to spot his position, and after the first bullet from below hit the ceiling, Levchuk slid down the ladder into the shed. *Let them shoot,* Levchuk thought. *It's a big shed and it's not so easy to hit anyone in it.*

He lay down near Klava. Two more shots came from the lean-to, and then everything grew still again.

"Hey, you! Still alive?" called Kudryavstev. "Stop wasting your bullets! Hand over the radio operator and get the hell out of there! Hear me?"

In the oppressive silence that followed the heavy round of firing, these words had an ominous ring. Levchuk did not reply, and nothing more was heard. Probably they were waiting for an answer. It was hard to know why they wanted Klava, and how they knew she was here. But obviously they knew. . . . Then Levchuk realized that she was precisely the reason they had come. And he, fool that he was, had hoped, had counted on getting some kind of lucky break. He should have cut them down at once with a burst of fire. Perhaps fewer of them would have been left to fight. But what could they do now?

Klava had put the baby down on the straw and had begun to cry. "Oh, God! Oh! What are we going to do?"

"Hey, you! Come and get your radio operator! Come on! Come and get her!"

He aimed his gun and fired through a crack— fired only once. He couldn't waste his ammunition. But that one shot was enough for them.

"Okay, you bastard!" shouted Kudryavstev. "Just wait! We're going to roast you like a pig in straw!"

12

Levchuk realized that this was no empty threat, that it was precisely what they intended to do. Obviously, to burn down the shed with them in it was something the *Polizei* would enjoy doing, but to do it they'd have to come close. And so Levchuk decided not to let them get anywhere near the shed, to fight them off to the last. He had a Luger and a handful of cartridges, Griboyed still had a couple of cartridge clips, and Klava had five bullets. They might be able to hold out until nightfall. Night was just what they needed—they might be able to break out in the darkness. But the sun, damn it, was still high in the heavens. They had a long way to go until nightfall, and waiting for it was going to seem like waiting for the war to end.

"Griboyed! Keep a sharp lookout! If anyone creeps up, shoot!"

He figured they'd probably killed two of them, maybe even three. From the sound of the firing, it was hard to tell how many were left. Two were stationed by the corner of the lean-to, one was hiding in the alder thickets, and one was undoubtedly waiting in ambush in the rye. The other fellow there wouldn't be getting up again. If they tried their hardest, they might be able to knock off another two, and if the *Polizei* didn't get any reinforcements, by evening their numbers would be equal. Then they'd see who'd win out.

Levchuk kept watch on the side near the thickets, which seemed to him the most dangerous place now. He imagined that one of them would try to crawl out from there and set fire to the shed with a torch. Or they might start by setting fire to the lean-to. He had no way of knowing which way the wind was blowing and where the fire might spread. But he was more alert than ever, determined not to allow anyone near the place.

When a shot rang out from the lean-to, and he saw the bullet flash under the rafters and go out the other side of the roof, Levchuk wasn't the least bit alarmed, thinking it was a tracer bullet. Another shot followed, leaving no trace, and he decided it was an ordinary bullet. Only when the third shot came did he realize what they were up to, and he went wild with fury.

They were firing incendiary bullets.

Klava was still lying on her side by the wall, shielding the baby with her body, while Griboyed remained by his crack in the corner. They weren't aware of what was happening yet, and Levchuk didn't tell them. He waited for the roof to catch fire, helpless to do anything about it.

He didn't have to wait long. After three or four shots, smoke began to curl into the shed. Klava was the first to see it. She glanced upward and let out a muffled cry.

"Levchuk! Levchuk!"

"Quiet! Wait! Be quiet!"

He himself had no idea what they were waiting for. For the first few minutes he simply watched as the eaves at one end caught fire, and the shed began to fill with smoke. First a small hole burned through the straw of the roof; then the flames quickly shot upward and to the sides. Gathering momentum, the fire began to crackle and buzz, devouring the dry straw; ashes and cinders came down on their heads. Griboyed was forced to leave his corner and move closer to the door; Klava, too, headed there with the baby. Levchuk remained where he was, glancing through his crack every now and then.

The clouds of smoke piling up in the shed were making it difficult to breath, and Levchuk imagined what it would be like when the whole roof caught fire. "Klava, into the drying room!" he shouted. "Quick!"

Klava needed no urging. She moved quickly over the high threshold, and Griboyed slammed the door shut behind her.

"We're done for, eh?" asked Griboyed. He looked distraught, and his eyes were reddened by smoke.

"Let *them* be done for," said Levchuk.

He wracked his brain, trying to think of a means of escape. To run out of the shed while the *Polizei* were guarding it on all four sides was madness. But they couldn't remain here much longer.

Two rafters at the corner of the shed burned through and collapsed, sending up a shower of sparks. Griboyed jerked his bare feet away. Levchuk, barely managing to dodge the fire, kicked a burning stick away with his boot, and raced for the door.

"Now we'll all burn together," Griboyed said grimly, and he began to cough.

Yes, Levchuk thought, *it looks as though we might.* But before that happened, they'd have to do something, or at least try to. If they failed, then they'd have no choice but to burn.

"Griboyed!" he cried, also beginning to cough. "The door! Give it a push!"

Griboyed reached out and pushed one panel of the door. It opened a little, and immediately two shots rang out from the lean-to. Two holes appeared in the thin boards of the door.

"Damn them!"

They had no alternative—they had to get out of this hell, and the only way out was through that door. One whole end of the shed was ablaze now. Flames were crackling and hissing overhead, the straw had practically burned right through, the rafters and the roof beams were blazing, tongues of flames slithering across them. Levchuk suddenly became aware that the backs of his trousers had caught fire, and he just managed to extinguish the flames by rolling on the floor. The door to the drying room burst open and Klava tumbled over the threshold, coughing convulsively.

"I can't stand it! I can't stand it any longer, Levchuk! I'm going to surrender! Save the baby!"

"Shut up!" Levchuk shouted. "Crawl over here!"

Still coughing, she struggled over to the door with the baby in her arms, and Levchuk moved aside to make room for her. One panel of the door was slightly open, and the wind beat against it and whirled the smoke everywhere, so that it was hard to tell whether it was coming in or going out of the shed. Levchuk reached out and pushed the door open wider with his submachine gun. One shot rang out, and then another. The first bullet struck near the door hinge and split the frame; the second apparently missed. Levchuk shouted to Griboyed to hold the door so that it wouldn't shut, and nodded to Klava.

"Get going! Hear? Duck in among the raspberry canes! And then head for the rye field."

She raised her tearstained face to him and, clutching the baby to her breast, stared at him for a few seconds, fearing or perhaps not understanding his intention. But time was running out on them. The entire roof was blazing, and the fire had moved lower—it was attacking the walls of the shed. It was so hot that it seemed they themselves would burn any minute.

Levchuk pushed her resolutely toward the door. Pulling herself together, and, after a second's hesitation, she slipped sideways through the open door into the raspberry canes. Levchuk expected a shot, but the *Polizei* were too slow.

"Griboyed, shoot! Out into the yard!" Levchuk shouted. And, at the risk of getting burned or of suffocating in the smoke, he raced up the ladder into the loft. He had to give her some covering fire from above, to keep them from shooting at the shed or intercepting her in the rye. He wasn't sure how to help her and he didn't even know how much ammunition he had left, but he raced under the blazing roof to the hole he had shot through earlier.

The rye field below was blanketed with smoke. Gasping for breath, his vision blurred, Levchuk shot a glance over the field. He saw no sign of Klava. Either she'd been shot down among the raspberry canes, or she had managed to flee the shed and hide in the rye. Indeed, two dark figures at the edge of the alder thickets were shooting into the smoke. Taking a gulp of air, he turned his submachine gun on them. He blasted them with everything he had left in the magazine, then took another gulp of the burning air and realized that he was choking. Everything was going black before his eyes; he was afraid he would pass out. He grabbed hold of a beam with his left hand, and hurled himself out into the raspberry canes.

He struck his thigh badly against a stone but jumped up at once, aware that a bullet had ricocheted right under his arm. It seemed not to have hurt him, and he ran, crouching, into the rye. Here he found himself smothered by the hot smoke. He began choking again, but he didn't dare to stop running—away from the fire, away from the shed, where the shooting had intensified and the *Polizei* had probably closed in.

Several fiery green tracers swept through the smoke as he darted deeper into the field. The smoke had thinned out here, and it trailed over the rye like a stifling mist. Crouching, Levchuk kept moving. Shots came from behind, even shouts, but he paid no attention. He had to reach the woods as fast as possible—there was no refuge for him in the field.

He moved across one divide and then another, crouching all the while, stumbling, then scrambling up, using his hands to help him move. He had long since stopped paying any attention to the pain in his right shoulder, and merely gritted his teeth when it got particularly bad. He had lost his cap somewhere, and sweat was pouring down his forehead and cheeks and, together with the smoke, was stinging his eyes.

Then the firing let up, seemed about to stop, and Levchuk thought he had escaped. All he had to do was get to the alder thickets.

He ran out of the rye field, then immediately darted back. But it was too late. Two men were coming to intercept him. Catching sight of him, the one in front dropped down on one knee and fired. Crouching as low as he could, Levchuk ran back into the rye.

Soon, however, the rye ended in a marshy meadow filled with tall grass and sedge. Beyond it was another field. But there was no point in racing for that field; they could easily gun him down there. His strength was practically gone, and his lungs couldn't get enough air. He took his pistol out of its holster and smacked the first cartridge into the breech.

Glancing up out of the rye, Levchuk caught sight of his pursuers' black field caps and shot twice in succession. The caps disappeared. He glanced up again, and when the first cap reappeared over the rye, he fired again. Then, pistol in hand, he set out along the edge of the meadow. If he could skirt it, he might be able to cut back diagonally to the alder thickets.

As he fled, he felt that he was not going to make it, that at any moment the *Polizei* would leap out of the rye and get him. He grew weaker and weaker, and his steps became shorter; his legs began to buckle under him. He was afraid he would fall— then it would be all over.

He looked back when a shot rang out from behind and a bullet passed low overhead. But he didn't quicken his pace; on the contrary, he slowed almost to a walk. His pursuer stopped at the edge of the field, shot from a standing position, then reloaded his carbine and dropped down on one knee, bracing his elbow against the other knee. That way, of course, he could take better aim, could be sure to hit him. But even then Levchuk didn't break into a run. He lacked the strength, and something in him revolted at this incessant battle for life. Under his breath he muttered, "Shoot, you dog!" And then he dragged himself, totally exhausted, into the alder thicket.

The *Polizist* fired. The bullet knicked some black turf under Levchuk's foot and ricocheted into the sky. "Go on! Shoot!" he shouted without looking back and staggered on.

The sound of the next shot reached him a moment after the bullet had whipped through the hem of his jacket and several of his cartridges had spilled onto the ground. He clutched his pocket in fright, as though the cartridges were worth more to him now than his own life, and quickly gathered them up.

He forced his way through a dense tangle of branches to a clearing and climbed up a pine-covered knoll. The forest began here. No one seemed to be pursuing him, but he walked on and on among the pines until he reached a warm, dry glade overgrown with whitish moss. He stumbled over a root and fell onto the soft moss, which was strewn with pine needles. Too weak even to turn on his side, he remained lying there flat on his face.

Meanwhile, the summer sky had begun to grow dim—the sun was setting. Cool shadows bathed the ground under the pine trees. Night was approaching. . . .

13

It was several hours before Levchuk came to. He sat up. Reality made itself felt in the boom of distant gunfire. He couldn't see anything, for it was night. His head drooped—and he longed to fall back on the moss and lie there. Listening to the sounds of the shooting, he concluded that the battle must be taking place some distance from the brushwood road, probably in the Krukov sector. Which meant that the May Day Brigade was getting its turn, that the mop-up expedition had gotten to them.

The events of the previous day drifted through his mind like a hot mist. The amazing thing was that he had escaped, had not been burned in the shed, had avoided a bullet, had fled into the forest, and was free now to go where he chose—except that this was of little comfort to him. He felt the stabbing pain of grief, of a great, irreparable loss; all his other emotions were stifled by it.

Levchuk sat up straighter and continued to listen. It was quiet nearby, as quiet as a deserted forest can be on a summer night. True, he heard numerous faint sounds and rustlings, but during his time as a partisan he had grown accustomed to the forest, and he knew that at night the human ear is too alert, that one imagines the majority of sounds he hears, and that the really suspicious ones reveal themselves clearly and immediately. Here the timid silence of the forest was broken by muffled gusts of wind in the treetops. Occasionally a dry branch fell, or the smaller birds fussed sleepily in the trees, but nothing else was audible.

As he listened to the firing in the distance, Levchuk decided he had best try to get to the May Day Brigade. Judging by all the signs, he would be able to get through only at night; the Germans would be sure to cut him off during the day.

Staggering, he rose to his feet and shifted his pistol from his stomach to his hip. His wounded shoulder ached. He supposed he should adjust the bandage, but decided he would do it in the morning. It was pitch black in the forest, and to avoid running into sharp branches or trees he had to grope ahead with his outstretched arm and bend his head. He remembered the route he had taken several hours before—he would have to get to the marshy area again and then go left along the edge of the forest. He didn't remember much about the rest of the area, but he hoped that the stars and the sound of the firing would guide him and he'd be able to stay on course. If only he didn't run into Germans.

For a long while he plodded through the darkness like a blind man, groping his way around trees and testing the ground with his feet to avoid stumbling against tree stumps and snags and growths of hard, impassable bracken. He kept his ear trained on the steady sounds of gunfire, but he was more preoccupied with finding his way and with thoughts about the threshing shed. He was tormented by the question of what had happened to Klava and Griboyed. Griboyed had probably remained in the shed—he would hardly have had a chance to escape through the door. But what on earth had become of Klava? It was as if she had vanished into thin air after slipping out of the shed—he'd seen no sign of her anywhere.

Suddenly he became aware that he was not moving in the direction of the shooting, but was retracing the route he had taken in the evening, but he didn't turn around. For now he realized that he had to go back there, to the shed.

Levchuk suddenly experienced a sense of acute impatience. He paid no more attention to the bushes and snags, and almost ran through the dark forest. He trembled all over as he relived the experiences of the day before. He felt certain that he should not have left Griboyed and Klava. True, he had no idea precisely what he should have done; he had tried his best to save her, and Griboyed, and himself too. But his belated feeling of guilt intensified, and he felt that he definitely must have done something wrong, because it seemed unlikely that anyone else had come out of that firetrap alive.

He scrambled out of the alder thickets near the very place where he had entered them the day before, and the rustling of the branches behind him ceased. Over the quiet meadow hung a whitish summer sky; a few stars and the misty edge of the Milky Way were visible. Grasshoppers chirped peacefully in the meadow grass, and ahead he caught a glimmer of the edge of the rye field where he had almost met his end. The threshing shed must be close by.

Levchuk paused briefly and held his breath. Apparently the *Polizei* had cleared out; in any case, it was hardly likely that they'd be waiting for him here. But to prepare himself for any eventuality, he quietly withdrew his pistol from its holster and pushed the safety catch off with his thumb.

He had expected to see some sign of the fire—but all he could see through the mist was the dimness of the rye field.

Suddenly he stumbled into a pit and almost fell. As he scrambled out, he spotted a thin gleam of fire through the branches of a bush. It seemed to be a long way off—it was just a reddish glow above the rye and gave off no light. Levchuk crouched quietly under the bush. It seemed there was no one around.

Cautiously, by stages, he moved closer to the shed.

Then Levchuk halted and stared in amazement. It was hard to recognize the shed. It was half the height it had been yesterday—the upper beams had burned completely. The lower parts were all charred, and in places embers would continue to glow as they were fanned by the wind.

He was still hoping to find Klava somewhere, but there wasn't a sign of her. He decided that she couldn't have remained here—dead or alive they would have found her and taken her back to the village. Griboyed too. But Levchuk wanted to convince himself that neither of them had remained. Only then would he set out for the May Day Brigade.

Levchuk had a view of the whole yard, where they had boiled potatoes yesterday; he could even spot a black patch that his fire had left in the grass. Opposite him was the door to the shed. One half of it, charred and riddled with bullet holes, was hanging crookedly on its lower hinge; the other half had been torn off and was lying on the ground. Near it, Levchuk noticed something that looked like a human body, and he darted out from behind the crab apple tree. Trying not to make any noise with his boots, he ran over to the door and squatted down. He groped with his left hand until it landed on something wet and sticky, and he pulled it back in revulsion. But when he tried a second time, he touched Griboyed's hairy, bloodstained face and charred clothing.

He stood up. The fetid smell and the smoke of the dying fire were suffocating. After taking a breath, he leaned over and groped further with his hand, trying to find Griboyed's rifle. But instead his hand landed on the man's sheepskin cap.

With the cap in his hand, he walked about ten feet away from the shed, unable to tear his gaze from the dark figure of the dead man. Levchuk had known him in the detachment for a long time. They had taken the same risks, and now Griboyed was lying here dead while he himself had remained alive. *Perhaps I should have tried to save him first and then myself,* Levchuk thought. But both of them had been trying to save Klava then. Instead, by some lucky chance, Levchuk had been saved, while Griboyed had died here.

His cap, however, had remained intact, hadn't even been scorched. It had been patched together out of an old piece of sheepskin and had served him winter and summer, for Griboyed had once been shot in the head, and afterward always wore the heavy cap to protect it. This time it had failed.

After mourning silently over the dead man, Levchuk decided that he ought to take Griboyed's charred body and bury it in the forest. It wasn't right to leave his body smoldering in this wreckage.

Keeping his ear trained on the stillness, Levchuk shoved his pistol back into its holster and walked over to the door again. But just as he was bending over the dead man's body, a dog began barking wildly not far away, and a flare soared up over the burned-out village. Taken by surprise, Levchuk shuddered and crouched as low as he could—but for a brief moment he was caught in the merciless glare. He leaped back at once and hid in the shade of the crab apple tree. The flare traced a fiery arc in the sky and had nearly reached the threshing shed when it fell, bounced on the ground, and then quickly burned out.

As soon as the flare went out, Levchuk dashed

back into the rye, wondering whether they had spotted him. A second flare went up in another spot—over the road and the forest—casting a triumphant glare over the wreckage of the fire, ruthlessly illuminating everything with its unnatural flickering light. This time Levchuk was ready for it, and he quickly flattened himself out in the rye. It wouldn't be so easy for them to spot him here. He wasn't afraid of flares, but he was afraid of Germans and the *Polizei*—and even more afraid of their dogs. The vicious barking of German shepherds was a sound all too familiar, and it terrified him.

When the second flare burned out, Levchuk jumped up and started to race through the rye toward the alder thickets. But something distracted him, and he crouched down again to look around. He thought he had heard a voice, something like the plaintive cry of a child, and he held his breath and listened. And then, more clearly than before, he heard the faint whimper of a child not too far off.

He hadn't a moment to lose. They were obviously closing in on him, the dogs might appear at any moment. He dashed on toward the alder thickets.

He probably would have made it into the alders had he not been cut off by a dense burst of tracer bullets that gleamed over the rye. To save himself, he dropped flat on the dry soil again and listened to the bullets crashing in the nearby bushes, mimicking the crackle of gunfire starting up in the distance. Now he knew for certain that they had spotted him and were firing at him from the road. Which meant that he would have to try to escape by the same circuitous route he had taken the afternoon before—through the rye, around the meadow, and into the alders.

As soon as the first burst of fire stopped, Levchuk leaped up. But before racing on, he made a half-circle in the rye, crouched, listened—and suddenly caught sight of a little white object on the ground a short distance away. With mixed feelings of bewilderment and hope he dashed for it, and, knowing now what it was, snatched up the live warm bundle, pressed it to his chest, and circled around further in the rye. He thought Klava might be lying here too, but there was no sign of her—only the baby, which by some miracle had survived. Levchuk ran on through the field.

"The swine! The swine!" he muttered, glancing back. He could hear the yelping of dogs fairly close behind him. They had doubtless picked up his scent, and at any moment might trap him.

He took cover in the alder thickets just before another flare shot into the sky, and a long crackling burst of high-speed bullets tore through the branches. Several tracer bullets flashed overhead, sprinkling Levchuk with wood splinters. He rolled over on his side, fearing that he would not get very far under this bombardment, and to escape with the child would be impossible. But he couldn't abandon him while the dogs were tearing after them. He just couldn't bring himself to do that. He did not know what the next few minutes would bring, so he plunged blindly into the thickets, pushing aside the branches with his left shoulder, and wrapping the hem of his jacket around the infant, who had snuggled down peacefully against the warmth of his body.

14

Daybreak found Levchuk on the edge of a deserted swamp in a sparse alder wood filled with grassy mounds.

The eastern part of the sky was filled with a remote, unearthly light that made it possible to discern the black crooked alder bushes, and the grassy marshland underfoot. He wondered if he had made any progress; he had been winding through marshy groves and clearings for some time. All through the night the barking of dogs had followed him—louder at some times, softer at others. The Germans had fallen behind in the darkness, but the dogs had not lost the scent, and now that it was morning they were sure to quicken their pace, to make up for lost time.

Levchuk held the warm little body awkwardly against his chest, and thought that if only he could find a village, farmstead, forester's hut, or simply a chance stranger in the woods, he would leave the baby—for no matter how hard he tried, he would never be able to save this life, there was no chance of it. The Germans had machine guns, dogs, and flares, and, yes, they must also have orders to kill him. And he, fool that he was, had thought he could break through to the May Day Brigade.

He ran wearily around the edge of the swamp, unable to decide whether to skirt it or get into the water. He still had a little time to spare, could still look for some refuge. Unless it became absolutely necessary, he did not want to step into that cold, murky water. The swamp must end somewhere, and he might be able to get around it.

But the swamp proved enormous. When Levchuk had run along its winding bank for about an hour, there was still no end in sight. The sounds of battle he had heard last night were to the right of him now, but occasional shots also came from the left and behind. It sounded as if there were fighting on all sides of him.

Under his jacket, the infant was beginning to fidget, to stretch and kick. Levchuk began to worry that it would start crying. It had no way of under-standing that unless they had a stroke of luck, they would soon be flattened out in the bushes, finished off by machine-gun fire. Or they might be mauled by the dogs, or captured . . .

Levchuk went on hoping that before the Germans caught up with him he would come across some kind people to whom he could give the infant. But the swamp really did seem endless. Ever since dawn there had been nothing but shrubs, meadows, willows, and alders—no villages anywhere in sight.

He desperately wanted to save the baby. It would be all too easy to leave it under a bush, and not have to answer to anyone for his action, but for precisely this reason Levchuk could not abandon the child. If he didn't save the baby, what was the point of this mad struggle for life?

"It's all right, little fellow," Levchuk murmured encouragingly. He scarcely recognized his own voice—he had grown hoarse from not speaking for so long.

Now the vicious yelping of the dogs had become much louder. As he listened to them approaching, Levchuk regretted that he didn't have a bit of to-bacco left in his pockets to sprinkle on his tracks. He realized that he'd have to climb into the swamp—he had no alternative.

The bank here was fairly high and firm, with

birch trees growing along the edge; the swamp re-
ceded a little off to one side. He ran about another
fifty steps and then doubled back. Levchuk found
a place where the marsh was overgrown and here
he took a long leap, trying not to leave too many
tracks on the bank, and scrambled toward a thick
willow bush.

Green hummocks overgrown with willows and
alders appeared between the pools of water. Holding
the infant against his chest, Levchuk moved hurriedly from hummock to hummock, grabbing hold
of branches with his left hand. Soon the slime and
murky peat covered him to his hips. *If only it doesn't
get any deeper,* he thought. *Otherwise, what am I
going to do with the baby?*

But the swamp did get noticeably deeper, the
hummocks fewer, and between them gleamed
stretches of dark water with no vegetation but some
water lilies. Levchuk knew that water lilies grew
in deep places, so he did not push on toward them,
but stayed close to the hummocks, where he could
grab hold of moss and branches. Once he thought
he heard a voice, something like a shout, and he
planted his feet squarely on the bottom and stood
still. But no more sounds reached him.

Finally Levchuk stopped at a mossy hummock,
leaned against it, carefully pulled off his jacket, and
wrapped the baby in it. The infant wriggled, but

instead of crying, it snuggled in silently against the warmth of the jacket.

"That's good. Now just lie quiet. The main thing is to lie quiet. Maybe we'll still make it."

Standing up to his hips in cold water, Levchuk looked around and tried to decide where to move next. It would be good if there were a fairly dry stretch of moss nearby, or an island where he could hide from the dogs and wait out the chase. But nothing like that was in sight. The swamp got deeper and deeper, the hummocks scarcer, and as he moved from one to the next, the risk of his going under increased with each minute. He held the bundle with the infant higher, carefully moving his feet along the bottom, sometimes slipping on the roots of bushes and water plants. At times he lost his balance and barely managed to keep above water, dragging up black hunks of mud from the bottom as he struggled to keep the baby dry.

The sun was well above the trees now, and for some reason there was no mist. A few scattered clouds appeared high in the morning sky, and for a moment it was very quiet. But suddenly Levchuk heard the angry barking of dogs, much louder than ever before.

He glanced back, frightened, realizing that they were already here, alongside the swamp. He was horrified to see that he had moved so little distance from the shore. He raced for the next hummock, where one branch of an alder bush dangled over the water.

As luck would have it, the hummock was in the deepest part of the swamp. Before he reached it, Levchuk had drenched himself completely, and had even gotten his jacket bundle slightly damp. He had also made too much noise; the Germans were close by now and might have heard him. To prepare for the worst, he placed the jacket with the infant in it on the mossy edge of the hummock, and, supporting the damp bundle with one hand, readied his pistol with the other. The water here came up to his chest. He hid his head behind the branch and waited, knowing that if they moved into the swamp with the dogs, he'd be sure to spot them first. If only the baby didn't start crying!

Actually, he heard them before he caught sight of them. A commander shouted something, and the branches of an alder bush near the bank began to sway. Levchuk ducked down deeper into the water and fixed his attention on a narrow strip along the bank that was not shielded by bushes.

The first to emerge from the thicket was a brown dog with reddish patches of fur on its sides. It was picking up the scent quickly, sniffing the ground and rapidly shifting its glance from one side to the other. Barely able to keep up with the dog, the

157

dog's master came dressed in the spotted camouflage suit and long-peaked cap worn by soldiers in German reconnaissance units. He was followed by another German, dressed the same way, who had a second dog on a long leash. They ran along the bank and had just gone into another clump of bushes when the rest of the rapacious pack came pouring out of the thicket onto the bank—ten men dressed in identical camouflage suits, armed with submachine guns, and equipped with field bags, water bottles, and binoculars. They spread out in a long line along the shore, running in Levchuk's tracks, glancing from side to side, prepared at any moment to take aim and unload their guns at him.

"Oh, you bastards!" Levchuk whispered through clenched teeth. Unless they ran on past the end of his tracks, he wouldn't be alive much longer.

He lost sight of them for a time as they moved among the alders, but he could hear the crackling of branches in the undergrowth, and he knew that any second now his fate would be sealed. Would they move on farther, or come back?

Soon he heard a confused yelp from one of the dogs, and then a shout in German. He surmised that the dogs had lost the scent. He lowered his shoulders into the water and leaned his head to one side, concealing himself behind the hummock. Then he glanced back. Beyond a broad stretch of dark water there was a dense willow bush where he could have better cover.

For a second he struggled with the reckless desire to race for the willow while it was still possible. But he restrained himself. Obviously the thing to do now was to sit tight.

No, they had not gone on—they were coming back.

They ran out of the bushes one after another. He gritted his teeth and stared at them, his heart pounding.

Just then Levchuk noticed the tracks he had left along the bank. There they were—a few very noticeable footprints in the shallows among the trampled rushes. God, how careless he'd been! If only they didn't notice, if only they went on and followed the dog! Numb with cold and tension, he watched one of them go past the footprints, then a second and a third. Finally the last one ran past—a fat, sluggish fellow with a sweaty, bloated face. Levchuk let himself take a deeper breath—perhaps he'd still make it.

His feet had sunk deep into mud, and as he freed them, he leaned his chest against the hummock and bent over the baby, who was stirring restlessly in his jacket. Levchuk lifted the hem—the infant was frowning, and Levchuk was terrified to think that it might start crying now. He plucked a stem of quince from the hummock and put it in the baby's mouth. *There, suck on that!* The baby actually began to smack its lips and grow quiet, and Levchuk figured that for the time being at least he had fooled the little fellow.

Then Levchuk became rigid with tension again. He could hear the Germans quarreling, and then heard a loud, demanding voice that was answered by someone so close by that Levchuk huddled down in the water again.

Suddenly a German appeared directly opposite him on the bank. The man had tied his bootlaces together and flung them around his neck, and, barefoot, he was following Levchuk's tracks into the swamp. Another German stood on the shore with his submachine gun at the ready. *"Forwerts, dort nicht tief!"**

*"Hier ist der Kluft,"*** the barefoot one grumbled, testing the water hesitantly with his feet.

Levchuk shifted the safety catch on his pistol with his thumb and placed the barrel on the lower branch of the alder bush. He decided not to let the German get any farther than the deep pool where the duckweed had been pulled apart. Then he'd shoot. This was one German who would not get out alive. The one on the bank certainly would

* "Go on, it's not deep there!" he cried.
** "There's a big drop here."

160

start shooting, but maybe Levchuk would be able to knock him off with a second shot. . . .

Now that Levchuk had formulated this plan, his fear vanished, his brain began to function clearly and precisely, and his hand became strong, capable of a direct hit. But the German, as though sensing that death was near, took his time. He moved ahead cautiously, lifting his thin white legs in their rolled-up trousers high above the water.

Come on, you scum! thought Levchuk.

Now the German stepped over to a curly bush of buckthorn and grabbed hold of a branch—but he slipped on the bottom and tumbled sideways into the water. As he tried to get up, he sank in even deeper and accidentally knocked off his cap, which drifted slowly away from him and then sank rapidly into the water. Having stirred up mud all around, the German raced back to the shore, angrily muttering something to his comrade, who was roaring with laughter.

The wet German, covered with slime, climbed out of the swamp and, still grumbling, stripped off his clothes until he was completely naked. He and his comrades went on for quite a while squeezing water out of the wet garments. Levchuk stood there watching, shivering, impatient for them to finish fooling around and get out of there.

Finally the German pulled on his trousers and

blue undershirt and began to put on his boots. Just then, a young, long-legged German with a flashlight hanging down his chest shouted something into the bushes. A voice answered him, and then Levchuk heard the bolt of a gun click loudly on the shore. There was a resounding burst from a submachine gun and bullets whistled over the swamp.

Levchuk couldn't understand where they were aiming. Certainly not at him—they were firing off into distance, where the rest of the group had gone with the dogs. Perhaps they had discovered someone else in the swamp? Perhaps they had turned up partisans? The Germans on the bank also headed in the direction of the shooting, the half-dressed one shifting his gun from hand to hand, hastily pulling on his tunic as he ran.

Levchuk decided this was his chance to move farther into the swamp, and he had just picked up the baby when another burst of fire sent water splashing high about him. He huddled over, pressing his chest against the moss of the hummock, and held the child against him. The Germans had arranged themselves on the shore like a pack of wolves once again and were riddling the swamp with submachine-gun fire.

So now they were going to shoot him down behind the hummock with a blind burst of fire, and he would sink quietly into the murky water of the swamp—not the best of all possible fates. It would be a good thing if they killed the little one along with him. For what if the baby was suddenly left here alone?

Disturbed by the shooting, the infant started to whimper. Levchuk pulled the folds of his jacket tighter around the tiny body. What if they heard him? Particularly the dogs? They had been barking wildly ever since the shooting had started; they were choking with zeal and probably eager to rush into the swamp. Maybe the thundering submachine guns had deafened both the dogs and the soldiers, so they couldn't hear the faint cries of the child.

Levchuk grimly watched dense streams of tracer bullets coming closer to his hummock. The Germans didn't begrudge their ammunition—they were shooting at every hummock, every clump of moss, every bush, every spindly tree in the swamp. Sprays of muddy water splashed up as the swamp seethed and surged under the impact. Foliage, small branches and rushes, and green duckweed were churned up with the water and went flying into the air. The trunks of the alder bushes were torn by bullets, and here and there white patches appeared on their black bark. Levchuk had never heard a barrage of fire like this, except perhaps in 1941, at the front near Kobrin. It was almost impossible to survive it.

He laid the baby down and wedged himself in behind the hummock, ducking as far down in the water as he could. It was a pity he couldn't also lower the baby into the water. Lying on the hummock, it was protected only by a little bit of moss. The baby would probably get hit first.

"Oh, you bastards!" Levchuk muttered.

On the open stretch of the bank he once again spotted the long-legged fellow with the flashlight dangling from his neck. He raised his submachine gun to his shoulder, and sent a long burst of fire across the swamp. Ten bullets alternating with tracers sent grass and moss flying into the air from the hummock closest to shore, then ripped the upper leaves off the alder bush on the next hummock.

The streams of bullets moved steadily closer to Levchuk. As though sensing his approaching death, the infant began to scream for all he was worth, but amid the clattering and thundering of the firing Levchuk could scarcely hear him. He was following the flashing of the tracer bullets, trying to figure out when his last moment would come.

Then three more Germans appeared on the bank, and another squall of bullets hurtled past Levchuk. With one hand Levchuk pushed the baby down into the moss as far as possible. With the other he aimed his pistol at the shore. He was determined to shoot at the last German, who had changed his magazine and was about to shoot another round.

But then, when he noticed that the Germans seemed to be firing into the air, that all their shots were going over his head and past him, he lowered the Luger. He glanced around quickly and saw that clumps of leaves were flying off the willow bush behind him, where he had wanted to hide just a short while before. They must think that was where he was!

He was seized with hope once again. He wrapped the baby more tightly, barely hearing its cry, merely sensing its feeble movements beneath his hand. *If only he doesn't suffocate,* Levchuk thought.

And now the shooting was clearly moving away from him. Probably the bastards figured they had shot up everything here. Fresh alder branches lay among the rushes, dense clumps of leaves floated in the water, and, a little way off, the bullet-riddled top of a birch tree was suspended over the water by a thin strip of bark.

Levchuk grabbed the infant and held it under his left arm; with his pistol in his right hand, he made his way quietly, trying not to splash, to the willow bush that had already been shot up. Surely they wouldn't bother to shoot at it a second time?

It was still possible to take cover under the willow, though the bullet-riddled bush had become noticeably thinner. Leaves and the white roots of water plants floated everywhere on the surface of the water, and weeds and green slime wreathed the mangled willow branches.

"Hush, little one. Be quiet for a bit," Levchuk said to the baby. He rested for a few minutes, looked around, and then moved on, farther into the swamp, bending in some places, forced to swim awkwardly in others, convinced that if the swamp didn't drown him this time, it might possibly save him.

15

About an hour and a half later Levchuk had left
the trees and bushes and the stretches of deep water
behind him. There were more and more areas with
grass and moss. In places the swamp was still deep
and the bottom unstable, but at least now he could
be sure of not drowning. He had stopped shivering
and was beginning to get warm. All he cared about
now was protecting the baby; he had ceased to
worry about himself. The worst, it seemed, was
gradually coming to an end—he had made it across
the swamp. Finally a row of fir trees loomed up
ahead like a dense wall. That meant he had reached
the bank of the swamp. But what awaited him on
that green shore?

At last he scrambled out of the swamp, and he made his way up a sandy slope overgrown with heather. His boots, still leaking, felt strange on dry ground. And he was not only wet from head to foot, but covered with slime. Pieces of water plants clung to his shoulders and sleeves, and the rest of his clothing was covered with duckweed and other green stuff. But the baby seemed not to have gotten too wet; its kicking and crying were probably due to hunger.

Levchuk ran, fearing now that the child might starve to death, unwilling to take the time to squeeze out his clothes or rest. He pushed his way through a dense thicket of firs, and found himself on a narrow but well-traveled forest path. *If there's a path, there must be a village nearby,* he thought with relief. *If only I don't run into Germans.*

He jogged wearily along the path for about ten minutes, and his motion gradually quieted the baby down until he was completely silent. Levchuk slowed to a walk. He was warm now, and he began to look around for a place where he could sit down and adjust his footwear. Probably there were no Germans here, and since there was no way of telling how far he had to go, he'd best rearrange his crumpled foot cloths right away, or he'd ruin his feet in his wet boots.

With this in mind, he started for some waist-high bracken near the path. But just then he heard the sound of voices nearby, and the clomping of hoofs. He darted off the path. Crouching behind a juniper bush, he waited breathlessly for the riders to pass. But the noise of the hoofs suddenly stopped, and a commanding voice shouted above his head, "Come out of there!"

Levchuk cursed inwardly. What now? Judging by the voice, the men were probably partisans. But how could he tell? They might be Germans or *Polizei*. Still clutching the child, he carefully drew his pistol out of his holster and leaned over the bush to take a peek.

They were right there—three men on horseback, all dressed partisan-style, in anything that came to hand. They were staring at the bracken and aiming their submachine guns at it—Soviet submachine guns!

"Hands up!"

Slowly Levchuk got up from behind the bush, leaving the baby on the ground and hiding his pistol behind his back.

His slow response evidently displeased the horsemen. One of them, a young fellow in an old faded field shirt, turned his horse resolutely toward the bushes.

"Drop your pistol! Come on! Hands up!"

"All right," said Levchuk in a conciliatory manner. "I'm one of you—what's all this about?"

"We'll see who's who!"

By now Levchuk was convinced he had indeed run into partisans. He didn't want to let go of his pistol, because he wasn't sure he'd get it back. He simply stood there, not quite knowing what to hope for.

"Look, he's just come out of the swamp!" said one of the men, a fellow with a pointed chin

"Hey, you're right!" said the first rider. He leaped out of his saddle into the bracken.

The third rider said nothing but stared at Levchuk. A broad-chested man in a gray, unbuttoned padded jacket, he looked older than the other two, and his face with its black mustache struck Levchuk as familiar.

"Wait!" he said. "Aren't you from the Geroisky sector? Levchuk's your name, isn't it?"

"Yes," said Levchuk, struggling to remember where he had met this man before.

"Then you must remember how we raided that junction? Remember how that section car blazed away at us?"

Levchuk remembered everything. It had happened last winter at a junction—he and this fellow with the mustache had dragged a sleeping car onto the rails in order to stop a section car that was coming down the track firing a machine gun. The

170

mustachioed fellow had lost one of his felt boots in the ditch and had been unable to push his bare foot through the deep snow to reach it. Both of them had nearly been killed by machine-gun fire.

With relief, Levchuk pushed his pistol back into its holster, while the two younger men slung their submachine guns over their shoulders, obviously feeling friendlier. The one with the mustache gazed at Levchuk with obvious interest.

"You did just come out of the swamp?"

"Yes," Levchuk answered simply, and he carefully lifted the infant out of the grass.

"And what's this?"

"This? A baby boy. It'd be a good thing if there were some women around here. He needs a mama. He's very little, and he hasn't eaten for a whole day."

The men remained silent, looking somewhat incredulous. Levchuk unfolded the jacket and showed them the infant's face.

"Wow! Really! Look at that! Where did you find him?"

"It's a long story. Look, we've got to find a woman. He's simply got to eat or he'll die."

"We'll give him to the family camp. There's one not far from here," said the young fellow in the field shirt. "Kulesh," he said, "take the baby from

Levchuk. You can take him to the camp and catch up with us later."

"No," said Levchuk. "I have to take him myself. Is it far?"

"It depends. It's a long way by road, but only ten minutes across the stream."

They moved out of the bushes onto the path. The horses stamped restlessly under their riders, who had evidently been hurrying somewhere. But they just couldn't leave this man from the swamp without any help.

"Okay, then!" said the man in the field shirt. Evidently he was the senior of the three. "Show him the way, Kulesh, and then catch up with us. We'll wait for you near Bort."

Kulesh, the one with the mustache, turned his horse, and Levchuk moved hastily along the path after him. He walked fast and tried to figure out which brigade he had encountered. Most likely it wasn't the May Day Brigade. Kulesh couldn't have been from that brigade when they'd done the job on the section car, because the May Day had been operating somewhere near Minsk then, and had only appeared in this area in spring. . . .

"Was it you the Germans were firing at in the swamp?" Kulesh asked, glancing at him from the saddle.

"Yes, me. I barely got away."

172

"I bet. That swamp's a bad one."

"Yeah, I thought I'd be sending up bubbles. You're in the Kirov Brigade now?" Levchuk inquired.

"Uh-huh, the Kirov," Kulesh replied. "The Germans have been giving it to us, the bastards. Hear that racket? We're beating them off."

Levchuk had already heard the rumbling of gunfire ahead of them. The firing was distant but heavy, and it sent booming echoes through the forest.

"Say, this little one isn't yours, by any chance, is it?" Kulesh asked, nodding at the bundle.

"No, not mine. A friend of mine," Levchuk said.

"Oh, I see."

"He'd hardly been born when he was left an orphan—no father or mother left now."

"That happens," sighed Kulesh. "Particularly now."

Levchuk walked on beside Kulesh's chestnut mare and gradually began to shake off the burden of all he'd been through. He had come out alive, and now it seemed fairly certain that he would save the baby. He looked around impatiently—would that camp never come into view? He wouldn't go any farther than the camp. He'd make arrangements for the baby there, get a good sleep, and then maybe go to see a doctor about his wounded shoulder. Wet, and never properly dressed, it alternately ached dully and burned terribly as though it were festering. What would he do if he got blood poisoning? The wound began to worry him more and more.

"It's not far now," said Kulesh. "We just have to cross the stream—the camp's over there."

Levchuk sighed wearily and glanced at the baby, who was napping quietly in his arms. Just as they reached the stream, they saw men rushing down the hill on the other side. They were armed and running in a disorderly fashion. One of them gestured with his arm, and Kulesh reined in his horse.

"What's going on?"

A dark-skinned man, with a harsh expression on his face, ran toward them. He was dressed in a German uniform, carried a German submachine gun in his hand, and had a huge pair of German binoculars dangling on his chest. Levchuk guessed that he was one of the commanders of the Kirov men.

"Kulesh, stop!" the commander shouted, slinging his submachine gun onto his shoulder. "Who's that?" he asked, eyeing Levchuk.

"He's from the Geroisky Brigade," Kulesh replied. "We're taking a baby to the family camp."

"What baby!" the commander shouted indignantly. "Into the line, both of you! The Germans have broken through. Don't you hear what's going on?"

"You want us to take a baby into the line?" Kulesh asked in amazement.

"All right, you take the child," the commander said impatiently. "And you," he said to Levchuk, "go into the line. Where's your rifle?"

"I don't have one," Levchuk said. "Here's my pistol."

"Take your pistol, then. Quick, follow me. March!"

Levchuk paused for a second, intending to say that he was wounded, but the excited faces of the commander and the men gathering on the path made him realize that it would be better to obey.

So he gave the child to Kulesh, who lifted it into the saddle with exaggerated care.

"The main thing is to get him to some woman, so she can feed him," Levchuk reminded him.

"I'll do that, don't worry."

The dark man with the fiery look in his eyes ran partway up the hill and glanced back. Levchuk, however, remained standing there, afraid that Kulesh might drop the baby. Kulesh dug his run-down heels into the mare's sides and took off, but wheeled back toward Levchuk.

"Hey, what's his name?"

"His name?" Levchuk asked, bewildered.

He was parting with the child forever, perhaps, and no one had given him a name. For that matter, had he himself thought about a name? He hadn't

even dared to hope the child might need one some-
day.

"Victor!" he shouted, suddenly recalling Platonov's first name. "Tell them it's Victor, and that
his last name is Platonov. If they ask—"

"Right!"

Kulesh galloped down the path and soon disappeared into the hazel grove, while Levchuk, shivering in his wet clothes, ran after the dark-skinned
man. As he moved along, he could hear the crack
of rifles and the first bullets whistling through the
morning air.

16

After a while, Levchuk began scanning the balconies, and somewhat belatedly guessed that the third one above the entrance was Victor's. To Levchuk's surprise, he also caught sight of a young woman in a light housecoat, who had stepped soundlessly onto the balcony. She watered some hanging plants with a glass jar, glanced down into the yard, and then silently disappeared into the apartment, leaving the balcony door open.

Levchuk went on sitting, unable at first to grasp the meaning of her appearance. She must be Victor's wife. That meant *he* was there. Out of the corner of his eye Levchuk had seen a couple with a little girl enter the building about a quarter of an hour before, but he had seen the man only from the back. He'd been of medium height, and had had a narrow build and thin elbows showing beneath the short sleeves of his shirt. Levchuk had paid no attention to him. In his imagination Victor Platonov was built differently, and so he had gone on sitting there, continuing to study each of the infrequent passersby. But apparently the time had come for him to get up.

Undoubtedly Victor would be different from what Levchuk had imagined. But in what way? He had to know because of all he'd been through. . . .

When the blockade was finally lifted, his arm was amputated, and he replaced Griboyed in the medical unit, looking after the horses. And what services could he perform tending the horses? So he cherished his memories of his past; his life had meaning because he had once saved a tiny baby from a pack of wolves.

After Kulesh took him down the path, Levchuk never saw the child again. He inquired about him whenever the chance arose, but no one was able to tell him anything. Who had the time to care about a baby when hundreds, thousands of sturdy men were being killed? . . .

Slowly overcoming a heaviness in his legs, Levchuk got up from the bench, picked up his suitcase, and walked over to the entrance. Suddenly he felt very nervous. He fought back an unpleasant surge of weakness in himself and slowly, pausing at times to rest, climbed the stairs to the third floor. The door to number fifty-two was still closed tight, but now he could hear people behind it. He pressed the doorbell and waited for someone to open the door. But instead he heard a low, good-natured voice call out, "Come in, it's not locked."

Forgetting to take off his cap, Levchuk turned the handle of the door.

ABOUT THE AUTHOR

A Belorussian prose writer, Vasil Bykov was born of peasant stock in 1924. He studied in an art academy and then in 1941 he volunteered to join the army serving on the front until the last day of the war.

The war theme became the main topic of each of Vasil Bykov's twelve books. Many other European countries and Japan have published translations of his work. In his own country he has been awarded the medal for "Laureate of the Government of the USSR," and a number of his novels have been made into movies and plays.

PACK OF WOLVES is Vasil Bykov's first novel to be published in the United States.

181